CW01497593

Pirched by the Krampus

SIGGY SHADE

Copyright © 2022 by Siggy Shade

All rights reserved.

No part of this book may be reproduced in any form or by any electronic or mechanical means, including information storage and retrieval systems, without written permission from the author, except for the use of brief quotations in a book review.

To all the monster lovers who like it big and bulbous and bursting with eggnog.

Trigger Warnings

Birched by the Krampus contains the following content:

- Abduction
- Body piercing
- Body modification
- Bondage
- Castration
- Corporal punishment
- Catfishing
- Evisceration
- Hell
- Humiliation
- Inflation fetish
- Magical torture
- Male entitlement
- Mentions of human sacrifices
- Mentions of punishing minors
- Object insertion
- Pregnancy
- Unprotected sex
- Water sports

harness around my chest to the empty basket around my back. I rattle my chains, making his lips tighten with disapproval.

"Krampus," he says, sounding weary. "How did you escape your quarters?"

"Blood ritual," I snap. "The elves guarding me made the mistake of being naughty. Now, step aside."

Klaus reaches into his pocket.

I step back, fully expecting him to extract a weapon, but he pulls out a large scroll.

My tongue flickers toward it and savors the ancient magic. "Is that—"

"The naughty list," Klaus says with a sigh.

Clutching the birch branches I fashioned into whipping rods, I take another step backward. This isn't like my sanctimonious brother. Where's the pleading to my better nature? Where's the begging on behalf of the 'innocent' children?

"You're allowing me to leave without a fight?" I ask.

"I'm afraid you were right all along. The world is a different place. All the naughty children I spared by keeping you locked up have become wicked adults, and they have spread evil across the land."

"Ha!"

Klaus opens the door, letting in a gust of frigid, ozone-scented air. My fur bristles and my tongue rolls back into my mouth.

It's been nearly a century since I've seen the snow, let alone felt the cold. I love the Northern Lights. The sky is a deep indigo, with streaks of mauve and cobalt.

My brother steps away from the open door and even sweeps a hand toward freedom.

"There has to be a catch," I mutter. "Do you plan on stabbing me the moment I turn my back?"

Chapter One

KRAMPUS

If my life wasn't linked to my twin brother's, I would eviscerate him with my claws then devour his entrails. Unfortunately, he is a deity, as am I.

Klaus stands at the doorway, brandishing a whip that's no doubt forged by his elves. He is everything I am not: handsome, suave, with flowing white hair and a matching beard. The smug bastard even wears a Hugh Hefner-style burgundy robe.

Most importantly, he looks human.

I stalk toward him, my fangs snapping, my hooves clicking on the wooden floor of our lodge. Tonight is December twenty-fourth, the one day in the year I have a purpose. The day I leave the North Pole to punish those on my naughty list.

Klaus has been my jailor for ninety years. Ninety years of sitting in a dungeon, watching the world go by in a scrying pool, while my brother hogged the spirit of Christmas for himself.

Narrowing his blue eyes, he glances from the leather

He raises his palms. "I can not object to your methods. Go forth and punish the wicked."

My hooves clop softly on the hard-packed snow. I study the distant mountains, inhaling the fresh, crisp air.

The only thing better than freedom would be a mate. Hell, those years spent in captivity would have flown by if I had a companion instead of bile and bitterness. No goddesses would look upon a creature like me with anything but disdain, and since human women are too small and fragile, I'll settle for punishing the wicked.

"Bardolph!" I yell.

The air fills with familiar grunts and snorts, and a dark figure emerges from the distant fir trees. My heart skips for the first time in nine decades at the prospect of seeing my steed.

Bardolph is large, even for a moose, standing eight feet tall with antlers nearly as wide. His fur is the same dark umber as mine, except his is far more luxuriant.

He charges at me, his eyes glowing red, and white foam spattering from his muzzle. Clouds of condensation stream from his nostrils, a fierce and glorious sight.

I raise a palm, ordering him to stop, and Bardolph makes a clicking sound in his throat and skids to a stop. He hangs his head low and snuffles my hand, his hot, moist breath warming my palms.

"You remember me," I say, my voice choked.

Bardolph grunts and nuzzles my shoulder.

"Are you ready for a night of mayhem?"

He lowers his head for me to mount.

I climb onto his back and pull on the reins. Bardolph turns around to position me in front of the doorway.

Klaus tosses the rolled-up naughty list. It unfurls before me, displaying my first victim:

NATALIA JASPER

An image forms in my mind of a brown-haired girl with freckles, cheating on an examination. Very naughty.

"I'm going to enjoy this," I snarl.

Klaus chortles from the doorway. "Oh, brother, I truly hope you do."

Chapter Two

NATALIA

I'm on my knees, unbuckling Stan's belt, my mouth salivating for a taste. It's not like me to meet men online, let alone invite them to my apartment, but it's been a lonely year. Online dating isn't the best way to meet wizards, but my line of work isn't very social. Technology is my family. Technology is my coven. So, a witch has to make do with what she can get.

Besides, his dick pics looked divine.

Long and thick and veiny, with a bead of precum glistening in the light of the camera. Once I saw what he was packing, it didn't matter whether he was ugly or handsome, old or young... I just wanted him here and now and in my mouth.

"That's it, sweetheart," Stan says with a groan. "Take it out. Choke on my huge cock."

Somewhere in the back of my mind, I note that Stan bears only a passing resemblance to how he looked online. Both versions of the man are blond with ruddy cheeks and hazel eyes, but the person standing in front of me is heavier with a less generous hairline.

He probably used a beautifying spell or one of the many filters available for witches and wizards to enhance their true appearance. Looks don't matter when a guy is well hung. Especially if he likes kinky shit like corporal punishment and bondage. Shoving away that thought, I yank down his zipper and reach into his silk boxers.

"That's it, baby," he rasps. "When we're done, I'll give you a nice spanking."

My fingers thread through a bird's nest of pubic hair, finding a shaft barely thicker than my thumb.

Snatching my hand away, I fall back onto my ass. "What the fuck is this?"

Stan looks down at me and frowns. "My cock, what else?"

Fury burns through my veins and heats my cheeks. It's directed more at myself for ignoring the first red flag—his altered appearance. If a man can conceal his weight and the state of his hair online, then of course he can lie about the size of his dick.

I'll be damned if I let that slide.

Scrambling to my feet, I stride across my bedroom and pick up the phone.

"Natalia?" he asks, having the nerve to sound confused.

I ignore his attempts to coax me back on my knees, log into the dating app, and open the inbox. My screen fills with the last of his dick pics.

The erection in the photo lies on a towel beside two cans of Magi-Cola stacked on top of each other. It's long and thick and juicy—just the way I like them.

He places a hand on my shoulder. "Natalia, what are you doing?"

I step out of his touch, brandishing the screen. "You told me that was your cock."

"It is," Stan says, his tone clipped and defensive. "And you promised to suck me dry."

A laugh huffs from my throat. It's harsh and full of bitterness. "Where did you get the cola? A doll house? You are the worst kind of dickfish."

He scowls. "What?"

"It's a catfish that uses fake dick pics."

Stan rears back, nearly tripping over the puddle of denim around his ankles, and hisses through his teeth. The man must be allergic to the truth. If he doesn't get out in the next minute, I'll electrocute him with my home security ward.

"I spent half my wages on membership, apps, new clothes, and a bottle of vintage wine," he says. "Now, you're complaining about the goods?"

My jaw drops. "Didn't you listen to a word I just said?"

He yanks down his boxers, exposing a dick shorter, thinner, and measlier than a lipstick vibrator. "Either suck me off or pay me what I spent on this date."

"Get out," I snap.

Sparks fly from his blond hair, making each strand stand on end. Looks like he was telling the truth about being a necromancer for the electricity guild. I clutch my phone and activate its emergency protection ward.

"Suck it." He reaches for my arm, only for his magic to backfire and hit him in the chest.

Stan stumbles back, and I advance on him with my phone. One press of my thumb activates the apartment's security wards, immobilizing him first before lifting him off his feet.

Ha. It serves that wanker right for underestimating my skills.

Stan flies into the fireplace, his face a rictus of terror amid a burst of flames and smoke. The air fills with the scent of burning hair before he's ejected up the chimney and out of my life.

"Merry Christmas and good riddance," I yell into the empty fireplace.

Ten seconds later, my phone chimes. It's an alert from the dating app. Stan's just invoiced me for the amount he's spent on the date, plus a significant sum for hurt feelings. At the bottom of the invoice is the warning in flashing capitals:

PAY UP IMMEDIATELY OR SUFFER MY CURSE.

"Yeah, right."

Stan must have prepared that shit in advance. I'd bet my entire month's salary that I'm not the first witch he's dickfished.

I slip the phone into my pocket and shake my head. "For once in my life, can't Santa send me someone who's better hung?"

Heat flares across the room. I spin toward the fireplace to find it filling with black flames.

My hand claps over my mouth. "Oh, shit."

A large hoof emerges from the fire, followed by another. They're cloven, looking like they belong to some kind of giant goat.

It looks like Stan wasn't bluffing about the curse.

Chapter Three

KRAMPUS

Flames singe my fur as I slide down the chimney. It's been such a long time since I practiced Christmas spells that I'm a little rusty at stealthy entrances. No matter. It will all come back to me once I have punished tonight's first victim.

I emerge from the flames, finding myself in a chamber that takes up an entire attic. From the spellbooks strewn across the wooden floor and the empty cauldron in the corner, it looks like Natalia Jasper is a witch.

Occult symbols glow crimson on the walls and ceiling: a pentagram, an inverted cross, and a six-sided star surrounded by flashing numerals. They fly at me before I can process what's happening, and form a barrier around my body, trapping me inside a circle.

I swipe at the ward with my claws, but they shift and move out of reach, leaving me to grapple with empty air. This is no ordinary magic. It is something unnatural and new.

Damnation.

I've only broken out of one prison, just to step into another.

Flashing my fangs, I glance around the darkened room. "Who dares to entrap the Krampus? Show yourself."

At the click of high heels, my attention snaps toward the corner bookcase, where a small figure steps out of the shadows, clad in a black dress that exposes her curvaceous thighs.

My gaze travels down to a pair of knee-length boots and flickers up to a heart-shaped face with painted red lips, high cheekbones, and eyes as green as the aurora borealis. Stunning, but nothing good will ever come from dwelling on the allure of a creature so delicate.

An ache forms in my chest, the way it always does when I think about women and the love that's been denied to me my entire life. I will soon work out that pain with my birch rods.

She must be the mother or older sister, trying to protect Natalia from my wrath. It will not work.

"What is the meaning of this?" I snarl. "Why have you imprisoned me in this circle?"

"I'm the one who asks the questions." She points a device at my chest that shoots lightning. Sparks fly across my fur but don't reach my skin. "What are you doing in my bedroom? The Magical Council already banished the Krampus."

Fury pulses through my veins. "How dare the mortals take credit for expelling a god?"

My rage picks up speed, fueling a wave of power that heats my chains. They rise off my chest, glowing a bright shade of crimson. As they reach the witch's barrier, the magic fades, and the symbols explode into red dust.

Free!

"Fuck!" The witch stumbles backward and points her device.

I swing the chain and slap it out of her hand.

"Where is Natalia Jasper?" I snarl.

"How did you know my name?"

My jaw drops, and I huff out a shocked breath as she sprints toward the door. No one on the naughty list should look so... mature. No one ever makes wishes to Klaus but children, and the magic that judges them never fails.

I raise a hand, summoning her with the magic of Christmas. She rises off her feet and floats back toward me, confirming that she is indeed Natalia.

"You're the first name on the naughty list." I grab her by the back of the neck and lift her to eye level.

Natalia's features tighten. "You can't punish me. The Krampus only comes to children. I'm twenty-one."

I stare into her pupils, the window to her soul, and see that she's telling the truth. "Twenty-one years, three months, and six days."

"Told you." She grips my hand with her slender little fingers. "Now, let me go."

"However, you attacked a god and the penalty for that infraction is death."

Her eyes widen, and she raises a hand. "Wait! There must be something I can do to appease you." She lowers her lashes and sweeps her gaze up and down my form, taking in the chains I wear across my chest. "After all, I didn't know I was dealing with the Krampus. My magic acted in self-defense."

As her fingers drift toward my fur, my skin tingles with anticipation of her touch. When was the last time someone reached out to me other than that bastard, Klaus? No woman has ever come into contact with my body and survived. My nerves thrum with worst sense of longing, even if the connection is only fleeting. I shove the sensation down into the pit of my stomach and growl.

Women never touch me unless it's to attack. They fight so hard to protect their children from being whipped, birched, or dragged to hell. A brave few have offered up their bodies instead, but I would never take advantage. It's hard to muster up any arousal for someone begging for the life of their offspring.

"Cease these distractions and take your punishment," I roar. "Or I will hand you over to Satan."

She snatches away her hand. "Alright. What do I have to do?"

My gaze darts around the chamber for a suitable surface. A polished wood desk takes up one side of the room. A flat metal item lies atop it, along with an earthenware pot containing wands and writing implements. I knock them to the floor with a sweep of my hand.

"Hey," she snaps. "That computer and tech belong to the guild."

"Silence." I shove her face-down on the tabletop and loop a length of chain around her wrists, securing her to the dcsk.

After kicking her feet apart, I bind her ankles to the table legs. She struggles, her back arching, but the chain tightens, keeping her immobile.

Perfect.

I step back to admire my handiwork. Natalia's legs are spread, the lean muscles of her hamstrings tightening with the stretch. My gaze travels up her thighs and to the black dress that barely covers her curvaceous ass.

A delectable sight.

Tightening my claws around the birch rods, I wait for the righteous indignation that always surges when I punish the naughty, wait for her to plead and cry and whine. Natalia isn't petulant or even repentant. She shivers and

16

sighs, as though I'm about to deliver something she will enjoy.

My brow furrows.

Natalia looks excited.

"You were frightened a moment ago," I say, my gaze narrowing at the way she tries to rock back and forth against the table. "Do you understand that I'm about to make you suffer?"

"Please," she replies, her voice hoarse.

I scratch the fur at the base of my horn. This is most unexpected. The chains have never gotten my victims into such a state of restlessness.

"Please what?" I ask. "Use your words like a good girl."

Natalia's breath quickens. "Please, Sir. Please punish me. I've been so bad."

Arousal surges straight to my cock, and it pushes painfully against its sheath. I groan, willing away the sensation.

"Foolish little witch. You should be terrified, not excited," I growl.

"If you wanted me scared, you shouldn't have bent me over that table," she snaps. "If you didn't want me so turned on, you shouldn't have started with the kinky bondage."

"Insolence!" I raise the birch rods and bring them down across her ass.

Natalia arches her back and moans. "Fuck!"

"Mind your language."

I bring the rods down once more, making her shudder and squirm. With each strike, her movements become more desperate until she ruts against the tabletop like a reindeer in heat.

My cock lengthens, thickens, and pushes against its hiding place until the ache makes me lightheaded. By now,

Natalia should be screaming for mercy. Instead, she's screaming for more.

Nobody could possibly enjoy this birching.

The more Natalia thrashes, the more her dress rides up and exposes her ass. Pink marks appear on her round globes, which deepen into delicious red welts. Delicious red welts I want to lick.

Saliva fills my mouth, and my tongue swells to the point that it hangs loose.

I can't stop. Despite my better judgment, I keep bringing the rods down, again and again, watching the darkening marks bloom across her skin. I don't stop until her entire ass is a masterpiece of delicate little bruises.

Still, she moans and thrusts back against the table, panting and trembling, her body arched and contorted against the chains. I've never seen anyone respond to a birching with such desire.

"P-please," she whines.

"What?" I hiss.

"Please, Sir. Give me more. I need it. I need you."

She elongates the last word with a siren's call that urges me to throw down the rods, unsheathe my cock, and take her hard and fast against the table.

My jaw clenches. No matter how much I want it, I cannot give in. No woman, not even a powerful little witch, could withstand my cock. Natalia is far too fragile.

Old memories rise to the surface, from the time of demigods and giants, when I fucked sacrifices until they were broken, bleeding, and begging.

I look down at the witch and see an echo of their hunger, an echo of my own in centuries past. I am no longer the devourer of women—I am that which punishes the wicked.

Natalia has no understanding of the creature I was

before I became the Krampus. I have no intention of letting her die.

Throwing down the birch rods, I grab Natalia by the hair. "Foolish little mortal. How dare you mock a god?"

Her breathy moan goes straight to my length. "I'm so fucking wet."

I release her hair, step back, and glance at the scrap of fabric between her ass cheeks.

It's soaked.

Damnation.

I should leave Natalia and move on to the next name on the naughty list. When I summon the parchment, her name doesn't dissolve. It remains at the top of the list and glows red.

Red can only mean one thing: Her punishment isn't yet complete.

Chapter Four

NATALIA

This is a witch's wet dream. Birched until my ass burns, and aroused beyond reason. My pussy quivers from each delicious strike, and my clit throbs in sync with my rapid pulse.

All I can do is lie on my desk and take this punishment. He's bound me so tightly to the wooden surface that I can barely move. I can only revel in the agonizing ecstasy of it — the way his strong hands mete out a perfect balance of pleasure and pain.

One strike hits my ass with a sting that my body registers as electric rapture. Vibrations travel down to my core and make my clit tingle. Then the next intensifies it until it overloads all my senses.

I clench my teeth and hiss, even though my breathing grows ragged.

The rods come down harder, swifter, each punishing blow coursing through my body with shocks of pleasure.

It's perfect agony, cruel ecstasy. I toss my head back, doing everything I can not to cry out, writhe, moan, and beg for more. But before I know it, my lips are forming the traitorous words.

"M-more," I rasp.

His voice rumbles, but there's a part of me that doesn't want to hear myself plead. But I'm so wet and needy and unable to focus.

When he yanks me up by the hair and pulls me off the desk, we finally lock eyes. His irises are a deep amber with fiery flecks that remind me of the furnace burning in my core.

Whatever I utter next has him sneering, baring a mouthful of sharp teeth. The blood roaring between my ears muffles his reply, but I'm sure it's something cruel.

He releases me, and I fall back onto the table with a whimper.

An eternity passes, long enough that my pulse slows, and the sensation between my legs subsides. His hoofbeats retreat, and I choke back a sob. Is he planning on leaving me unsatisfied?

"You must be an exceptionally naughty witch," he snarls.

My heart leaps. "Why?"

"The naughty list says you need more correction."

"Yes." I buck my hips. "More. Please."

A rolling growl sounds from behind me, making every fine hair on my body stand on end. It's so thunderous and deep and feral that I can't help wondering if my begging has awoken something primal.

Hoofbeats approach, each strike on the wooden floorboards hitting my eardrums like percussion. The sensation trickles down my nerves and concentrates on my clit.

He stops behind me, where I'm still bent over with my legs spread. A cool draft wraps around my exposed legs, making my skin prickle with goosebumps. I lift myself onto my tiptoes, the movement spreading my pussy lips.

"Look at you," he says, his baritone resonating through my needy core.

Krampus steps closer until my skin tingles with his magic. I swear I can feel the tips of his fur brushing against my skin.

His hot breath tickles my neck, infusing my veins with a delicious thrill. Then he wraps a calloused hand around one wrist and then the other and pulls me upright.

The chains around my wrists clink as he shoves me to the floor. I fall on my hands and knees with a cry.

"No one on the naughty list may enjoy the punishment, but you have defied me at every turn." When I try to raise my head, he shoves me back down with a roar. "Cease your defiance and kneel before the Krampus, or I will cast you to hell."

I curl my hands into fists. There's no point in mentioning that the Council of Magic already closed that loophole. Every wizard or witch is tattooed with sigils that prevent forcible transportation across realms. But who knows if that protection will work with Krampus?

Best not to test a creature who claims to be an old god.

"It's not my fault," I say from between clenched teeth. "You shouldn't make the punishments so kinky."

He grabs my hair again, this time to force our gazes to meet. "Explain."

The fiery flecks in his eyes brighten, and he flashes me his fangs. Shit. My throat tightens. Will he freak out if I tell him about BDSM? I can't even think of an appropriate lie.

"Listen, I'm sorry for attacking. I thought you were someone else."

His eyes narrow, and I swear I can hear the beginning of a warning growl. If I don't get to the point, he'll do something I won't enjoy.

"Some adult witches enjoy a bit of BDSM," I blurt.

"What?" he hisses.

"Bondage, dominance, submission... er... sado-masochism?"

Krampus stands so close that I can feel the force of his rage. I hold my breath, waiting for him to make a move. Maybe he can't. Most of these old gods are only good for one thing, such as fertilizing the land, making thunder, and punishing naughty children.

My gaze drops to the thicket of fur between his legs. Maybe the Krampus doesn't have a cock?

"Are you serious?" he asks.

"Y-yes." I stutter, my heart pounding to the throbbing of my clit. "Some of us like pain."

"What happens after a BDSM punishment?" he rasps.

It takes a few seconds to register what Krampus is asking. There's no way I can tell him it's a sex thing... Can I?

"Tell me." His hand tightens in my hair, sending shock-waves of sensation down my spine. "I will know if you're lying."

"Then we fuck."

Silence.

My stomach drops. It's about this time I remember that some people are squeamish about sex. I expect that the god of Christmas retribution would be horrified. In a minute, he'll consign me to hell, or if that doesn't work, I'll be dead.

"Or I suck his cock?" I blurt.

His pupils widen. They're horizontal as if I didn't need any further reminder that he's a monster. A monster I've now scandalized.

"You enjoy this activity?" he asks, his voice guarded.

There's no point in making myself sound innocent. Krampus probably wasn't bluffing when he said he could tell if I was lying. "Oral sex is only worthwhile if the cock is long and thick."

"And human-shaped?" he says with a sneer.

I flick my head toward my bed, where I keep a selection of toys on the nightstand. "The more unusual the better."

As Krampus turns his head, I consider scrambling to my feet and making my escape, but the weight of the chains around my wrists and ankles reminds me I won't get far.

His huge chest rises and falls as he surveys the tentacle grinder, four-headed rubber dildo, and fox-tailed butt plug.

"What a peculiar little creature you are," he murmurs, his gaze fixing on mine. All the bite in his voice is gone, replaced with something akin to wonder. "Arousal from pain sounds like a contradiction."

"Not for me. I've always liked it rough."

His sneer returns. "A puny little witch like you couldn't last a minute with a god, especially one of my immense girth."

Girth?

Heat floods my pussy, making my clit swell. I sweep my gaze up and down his seven-foot form, taking in the way his fur clings to his thick, ropey muscles. If his cock is in any kind of proportion to his size, then I'm screwed.

In more ways than one.

Fuck.

He snorts. "Pah! You'd be a whimpering mess."

"I'm tougher than I look." My tongue darts out to lick my lips. "Try me."

Silence stretches across the room, save for the frantic beat of my heart. Arousal trickles down my inner thigh, setting off a flurry of sensations that make me squeeze my legs together.

A little voice in the back of my head whispers that this is a mistake. I should beg for forgiveness, take the rest of my punishment, and make do with my toy collection, but it's been a year since I've had a decent-sized cock.

Somehow, I don't think Krampus will disappoint.

"Very well," he rumbles. "I will commute the rest of your punishment to two hours with me. If you can survive, then I'll erase you from the naughty list."

Movement flashes in the corner of my eye, and I glance down to find the longest, thickest, reddest cock, standing to attention.

And it's shaped like an upside-down Christmas stocking.

Chapter Five

NATALIA

My breath catches, and heat shoots straight to my core. The slickness between my legs intensifies, and even more arousal trickles down my inner thighs.

Who would have thought that I would have a monster kink?

His cock is thicker than my bicep, adorned with prominent veins along an impossibly long shaft. It's probably the length of my forearm, but it's hard to tell since it bends forward about two-thirds of the way up and ends with a bulbous head the size of my fist.

Shit.

He's too big. That monstrous cock will never fit.

A pearlescent bead of precum at its slit glistens like a Christmas bauble, and I salivate for a taste.

"May I touch it?" I whisper, my fingers trembling.

"You have not earned the honor," he rumbles.

The chains around my wrist tighten, jerking my arms behind my back and pulling so tightly that my chest pushes forward. The lace of my bra presses against my nipples, making me groan.

How the fuck am I going to touch myself if my hands are bound?

His voice cuts through my thoughts. "Suck, little witch. Show me how you pleasure a god."

His deep voice sends shivers down my spine, and I lick my lips, searching for what to say.

"Yes, sir," I murmur, knowing full well I'm in way over my head.

Then, I lean forward and run the flat of my tongue up his slit, finally getting a taste of his precum. It's sweet and creamy, with hints of nutmeg, vanilla... cinnamon, and bourbon.

"Is that... eggnog?" I ask with a gasp.

He groans, his hips jerking forward. "Cease your chatter, little witch, and choke on my cock."

I swirl my tongue, licking and teasing him with slow, tantalizing strokes that make him shiver. He might be high and mighty and infused with ancient magic, but he's still a man—a man who can't deny my skill.

Sucking on his slick head, I scrape my teeth against the smooth flesh. He whimpers, his breath turning ragged.

"That's it, little witch. Show me what you can do."

I open my mouth as far as I can, then take him inch by delicious inch to the back of my throat. His cock is so big, so hard, it almost hurts.

Bobbing my head, I slide thick, luscious length up and down my tongue, making sure to explore every ridge and vein. This is incredible, and my arousal is almost too much to bear.

When I hollow my cheeks to create suction, he makes a satisfied growl that travels across my skin.

"Good girl," he rumbles. "You know exactly how to please a god."

I hum around my mouthful, enjoying how he shudders and jerks with every teasing lick.

His hips rock back and forth, more gently than I expect from one so powerful, and soon I'm lost in the pleasure.

"Fuck, little witch, where did you learn to suck cock? You're taking it so well."

I know better not to tell him about my size kink. Not that I've had anyone as impressive as him. All men like to think they're the first or one of few, and I expect the Krampus is no exception.

"You weren't joking when you said you liked your cocks long and thick," he says, "But were you telling the truth about liking it rough?"

Nodding, I try to form words, but it's impossible when the Krampus fills me so completely.

"Eyes on me," he growls.

My gaze flicks up to meet amber eyes that burn hotter than my fire and a grin just as bright. Pride swells in my chest at the thought of him being impressed. I suck harder, eager to earn his favor.

"Listen carefully, little witch. I'm going to fuck your throat, long and hard. Survive, and I will give you a reward."

I give him a sharp nod and mumble, "Do your worst."

He threads his fingers through my hair, gripping so tightly that every inch of my scalp tingles. As he pulls back, my stomach tightens with a mix of dread and excitement. Excitement that this is going to be the hottest and wildest experience in my life, and dread that it might be my last.

At least I'll die happy?

Shoving those thoughts aside, I swallow hard, preparing for the onslaught.

With a snap of his hips, Krampus pushes into me with a hard thrust, making me gag. I clench my fists and dig my nails into my palms to steady myself through his merciless pounding.

My eyes water and tears stream down my cheeks, as my clit throbs like an exposed nerve. If it wasn't for the magic thrumming through my system, I would probably suffocate. I'm so tiny compared to him, each powerful thrust leaves me so dizzy and breathless that I'm seeing double.

"Keep breathing," he says, sounding unusually concerned.

The Krampus slows, giving me the chance to comply, and he even pats my head like I'm his pet. As soon as I'm relaxed, he rewards me by picking up speed and ramming his cock in and out of my mouth.

"That's my girl," he rumbles.

The praise goes straight to my clit. I pinch my thighs together, my hips jerking in counterpoint to his thrusts, trying to create a little friction. My pussy is so slick that the effort is futile.

I have never in my twenty-one years of existence felt so aroused. In all the times I'd practiced with huge dildos, none of them had ever felt so intense.

Bobbing my head back and forth within his punishing grip, I try to match his movements. Right now, I wish my hands were free so I could climax. Even better would be the chance of him splitting me open with that monster dick.

His rhythm stutters and his face twists into the kind of grimace men make when trying to hold back.

Shit. I've brought him to the brink.

Without thinking, I moan around his cock, taking him even further.

"Get ready, little witch. I'm about to cum."

I nod, inhale the deepest breath, and try to relax my

throat as his thrusts quicken. My vision blurs, and I blink harder, faster, determined to watch his pleasure.

A few heartbeats later, his thigh muscles tighten, and he throws his head back and roars, flooding my mouth with warm, creamy fluid. It's rich and thick, tasting finer than alcoholic milk punch.

I keep my mouth sealed tight, swallowing in measured gulps, savoring every drop of his velvety cum, but there's so much fluid that rivulets spill down my chin.

Finally, after an eternity, his grip on my hair relaxes, and his thrusts slow. The Krampus withdraws, and I'm left panting, my body on fire. I gulp, expecting my throat to be raw, but it feels oddly relaxed, unlike the ache between my legs.

"Good girl. You did exceptionally well," he says, his voice infused with warmth.

Unable to speak through my gasping breaths, I offer a tiny smile, my skin burning with need.

He picks me up and cradles me in his strong arms. His fur is warm and dense, almost like a mattress. It's so comfortable, I could lie here for an eternity.

With a gentle hand, he wipes the semen from my chin, then plants a kiss on my forehead. An ache forms in my chest. When was the last time a man showed me any affection? Certainly not at the Council's foster home.

And there are no covens with tech witches, just a guild that offers online seminars and quarterly meetups that hardly anyone attends.

"I expect you're wondering about your reward." He carries me to the other side of the room.

Nodding, I lick my lips and don't bother to ask why he's taking me to the fireplace. I rest my head on his furry shoulder, feeling so safe in his tight embrace that I wouldn't care if this creature took me back to the North Pole.

"Let's get you cleaned up." He settles me on the mantelpiece, sending a sting across my sore ass cheeks, and parts my thighs. "Look at you, all swollen and wet."

I whimper, still breathless from sucking his humongous cock.

"Would you like me to lick that pretty pussy clean?"

Chapter Six

KRAMPUS

There must be something wrong with this witch. Not only did Natalia not recoil from my bent cock, but she survived it. Fuck. When I climaxed, she couldn't get enough of my cum.

My cock stirs at the memory of those tight throat muscles, squeezing its tip to the point of pain, milking me of every drop. Could Natalia be different from all the others? She is a strong little witch with a huge appetite, but could she possibly be interested in more?

"Oh," she says, her voice breathy. "That was hot."

Every ounce of my attention switches to her pretty face. Her eyes are half-closed, her lips swollen and scarlet and smudged. Natalia looks scandalously debauched, but not yet satisfied.

She splays her legs, revealing a pussy that's dripping wet. Arousal surges through my veins. She looks like an offering. An offering willing to give her life for one night of pleasure and a year of fruitful harvests.

My throat constricts. I step back, keeping her at a distance of two feet. At a time like this, when I have a willing woman begging for my touch, I should not be thinking about the past.

I push the feeling aside and focus on the squirming little witch.

"P-please," she says with a whimper. "I need your tongue."

"Show me where," I hiss.

She bucks her hips, displaying a pussy so glistening wet that my tongue unrolls itself and drifts toward her swollen clit.

Her eyes go round, and her mouth falls open. "Your tongue... It's so long and thick."

"All the better to please you with, little witch."

In truth, I want to plunge it inside her until she squirts, then replace it with my hardening cock, but I can't risk her life. It no longer matters that I found Natalia on the Naughty List. She's a very, very good girl.

A good girl I need to savor, not slaughter.

The pointed tip of my tongue brushes the peak of her clit, making her twitch and moan. I take my time, making gentle circles around the sensitive little nub to draw out her pleasure.

She clings to the mantle, her legs trembling, her teeth worrying at her bottom lip. Each circling of my tongue elicits a panting little breath.

Natalia is utterly delicious.

Her scent fills my nostrils, a sweet mixture of arousal and peach that drives away my darkest thoughts. I flick my tongue over her swollen bud until her body convulses. Any more of this licking and my little witch will climax.

Taking the pressure off her clit, I move it down her slick folds and savor more her taste.

"Wait," she cries, her features dropping. "I was so close—"

"No cumming without permission," I growl.

She squeezes her eyes shut. "Please."

"Good witches get orgasms." I run my tongue up and down her dripping slit, gathering up her sweet juices. "Witches who complain suffer red bottoms and twitching clits."

Her mouth clicks shut.

"Good girl."

She makes a muffled moan, relaxes her thighs, and leans back against the wall, letting me explore her delectable pussy.

"Are you always so wet, little Natalia?"

She shakes her head.

My chest inflates with pride at the notion that only I can bring this beautiful creature to a state of such arousal. She sees my horns, my matted fur, and my long teeth, yet she hungers for my tongue.

"What do you want?"

"Fill me," she whispers.

"As you wish."

This is one wish I can fulfill, as I can fuck Natalia with my tongue without risking her life. Stepping forward to position myself directly between her spread thighs, I slide my tongue down her wet folds and to her tight little entrance.

The tapered tip slides in with ease, even though her walls clamp around it. I push further into her pussy, enjoying the textured ridges and crevices.

Pressing deeper, I find an interesting little spot. It's a little thicker, slightly rougher than the rest of her pussy, and I give it an experimental tickle with the tip of my tongue.

Natalia gasps, her hands clutching at the fur on my

shoulders. I glance up into her features to find them contorted with agony.

What in the Nine Hells have I done?

Chapter Seven

NATALIA

Pleasure courses through my pussy with the force of an electric storm, with lightning bolts of ecstasy thrumming through every nerve. My legs straighten before going rigid. Krampus's tongue lies still against the spot, but it's so sensitive that I feel the movement of its taste buds.

Whatever he did earlier—those gentle, teasing strokes on my g-spot—has triggered an avalanche of sensation that won't stop.

The most intense orgasm sweeps through my core, making its walls spasm around his thick tongue.

"W-what—"

Another wave of pleasure seizes my muscles, shoving every molecule of air from my lungs. I cling onto his shoulders, every inch of me clenching and shuddering.

I've never cum so quickly with a man or so hard, but I expect an old god like Krampus has had thousands of years practicing his techniques with women.

The orgasm intensifies until my vision fills with spots, and a little part of me already feels the pang of losing him. It was hard enough to find a man who can satisfy my size kink. Now, nobody could ever compare to Krampus.

"Natalia?" he asks, his voice thick.

Heat floods my system, burning my cheeks with an encroaching sense of embarrassment. He wants his tongue back, but my pussy won't let go. The contractions of this orgasm are so deep they border on pain.

"S-sorry." I flop forward, resting my head against one of his horns. "My climax won't stop."

"It's okay," he murmurs. "Let it take its course. There's no reason to fight it."

His huge, leathery palms run gentle strokes down my thighs, the touch as soothing as his voice. My chest tightens, and I don't know why the backs of my eyes prickle with the onset of tears.

Nobody has ever taken the time to learn my body. The first guy I ever slept with was so ineffective and small that I barely even got close to cumming. I tolerated the bland sex to stave off the loneliness, but even he ended up cheating.

Then there was another loser with an average-sized dick but was only interested in siphoning my magic. After that, it wasn't just my heart that I needed to guard. It was my power. Since the wizards I know aren't capable of love or even giving satisfaction, I decided to only have no-strings encounters with men who had big cocks.

"That's it, little witch," he growls. "Let it all out."

The orgasm continues, squeezing every ounce of pleasure from me until I'm melting into a puddle of bliss. As my muscles relax, the tiny movements of his tongue set off another flurry of fireworks.

When it's over, I collapse back against the wall and glance down at the Krampus through half-lidded eyes, panting and spent.

He gazes up at me with the kind of wonder I've only

seen on wizards making magical discoveries, as though he's never seen anyone cum so hard. I blink away that thought and dismiss the wishful thinking. An old god like Krampus probably has an entire temple of women, lining up for a chance to get pleasured by their lord.

"Are you alright?" He cups my cheek with his huge, leathery hand.

My eyelids flutter shut. "You found my g-spot," I reply through panting breaths. "I've never cum so hard."

The rumble of his deep chuckle goes straight to my clit. "You're a naughty little witch. I wasn't expecting multiple orgasms."

Neither was I.

It usually takes the tentacle grinder, a vibrating clit-tickler, and a few enchantments to get me to cum even half as hard, yet the Krampus did it with a few flicks of that clever tongue.

He swipes the pad of his thumb over my lip, making my eyes snap open to meet his amber eyes. Amber eyes that flicker with flames.

"That orgasm was most enjoyable for me to witness," he rumbles. "But I want you to give me one more."

"What?" I say with a nervous giggle. "I couldn't possibly—"

A rolling growl cuts off my words, making every inch of my skin tingle with anticipation.

"No arguments. When I let you down, you will lie on the rug with your legs spread and I will tongue your delectable little pussy until you squirt. Is that understood?"

"Y-yes, sir."

He slides a forearm beneath my legs and carries me down off the mantelpiece. As he settles me onto the wooden floorboards, warmth from the fire radiates on my ass.

I glance down at my pussy and bare thighs. Somewhere

between the birching and the intense cunnilingus, I must have lost my skirt. Not that I'll need it if the Krampus intends to lick me until I ejaculate.

Sparks fly from the fireplace, hitting my boots. I turn around, just as a flare of magic shoots out from the flames and yanks me off my feet.

I open my mouth to scream, but the sound gets lost in the crackle of the flames. Someone's dark magic enchantment has burrowed through my wards and is now dragging me up my own chimney.

Chapter Eight

KRAMPUS

A powerful blast of death magic shoves me across the room. My back hits a bookcase, sending books and trinkets flying.

I land on my hoofs, my mouth falling slack.

Was she taken? Impossible.

Her dwelling is protected by magical security.

Every hackle rises with indignation. If Natalia left, it had to be on purpose.

Had Natalia been pretending all along to want me? Was everything I enjoyed with her an elaborate trick so she could bide her time and escape? Old memories resurface of ancient sacrifices, of how no woman could have sex with me and live.

A witch as clever as Natalia had to know my weakness, my centuries-long desperation for companionship. A witch as beautiful as her would never stoop to sully herself with a creature like me out of choice. My jaw clenches, and I barrel toward the fireplace.

"Nobody takes advantage of the Krampus."

Just as I reach the hearth, the flames dim, and my passage is blocked by an invisible barrier.

"Damnation," I snarl.

The flames die, and the tiles making up the fireplace expand and meld together, forming what appears to be a solid wall.

"Natalia Jasper," I roar, "You will pay for giving me false hope!"

If she believes I'm trapped and won't be able to find her, she can think again. Contrary to what everybody believes, Klaus and I don't always require chimneys to enter an establishment. On December twenty-fourth, the magic of Christmas allows us easy access to all mortal dwellings.

The candles illuminating the rest of the attic room flicker, and I stalk toward the door, each footstep weighing down my heart with disappointment. They all leave me, whether it's via death, deception, or disintegration. A kaleidescope of images assault my mind of goddesses who laughed in my face, and priestesses who perished. I hadn't realized this until now, but Natalia was supposed to be different.

I reach for the door handle, but a jolt of lightning wraps around my fingers, making me hiss.

"You will not be my jailor," I snarl and lash at the door with my chains.

Sparks fly, but the attack fails to reach my fur. My rancor grows with each passing second. Natalia didn't have to go so far. She could have bargained for her release after sucking my cock. Instead, she chose to beg for more.

Enough.

I will not spend a moment longer wallowing in how I was tricked. Best to save my energy for catching up with Natalia and giving her a well-deserved spanking.

"Bardolph!"

Closing my eyes, I make a slow count to ten, blocking out unwanted memories of swollen lips, heavy-lidded eyes, and a glistening cunt.

The floorboards tremble with the approaching hoof-beats of my loyal moose. They stop at the other side of the door, filling the air with the sound of his panting breath.

"I have a mission for you, old friend," I say. "A powerful witch has imprisoned me behind dark wards."

Bardolph huffs.

"What do you mean, not again?" I snarl. "The last time, it was my bastard brother and his army of elves. How am I supposed to know the mortals have upgraded their magic?"

His snort of outrage for my predicament is welcome, if not overdue.

"Let us put your mighty antlers to work, shall we?"

Bardolph rams the door for the next minute or so, jostling the entire building. I pull out the Naughty List, finding Natalia's name still emblazoned in red. Apparently, the Christmas magic requires her to endure further punishment.

I thrash at the magical barrier with my chains, weakening it from the inside. With each strike, I think of ways I will chastise Natalia for her defiance. How will she like the paddle, the cane, the tawse?

She'll get all the pain she enjoys, all the sensations that will soak her pretty pussy, but I'll leave Natalia begging and aching to cum.

"That's right, little witch," I say, my attack on the barrier strengthening. "By the time I've finished with those red cheeks, you'll wish you'd never made it to the naughty list."

With an almighty crash, the door smashes into a mass of sparks and splinters, which brush harmlessly against my fur.

Bardolph stands in the middle of a darkened hallway, his

head turned to the side due to the immense span of his antlers.

"Good job, my friend."

I mount my trusted moose who trots down the passageway and into a hole he must have made in the wall to come to my aid.

"Did you see a little witch with my scent?" I ask.

Nodding, he leaps out of the hole into the space above a village square. Drunken shouts from drinking establishments echo along the parade of three-story buildings with snow-covercd roofs.

At this time of the night, children are all tucked in bed, with only ne'er-do-wells prowling the streets.

"You saw where she went?"

A scream pierces the air, making my head snap to the side. I recognize that cry, only this one is infinitely less lustful.

"Natalia!"

I pull on the reins, ordering Bardolph to gallop toward the direction of the sound. He lurches forward, his hoofs hitting the air with tiny thunderclaps.

My stomach tightens into painful knots. What if I was wrong about Natalia? I was so preoccupied with being rejected by her that I hadn't once considered that she might have been abducted.

Damnation.

If anything happens to her because I wallowed in self-pity, I'll—

Her second scream sends my blood to a roiling boil. What would anyone want with my witch? Bardolph descends behind the corner building, passing its garden of trees with skeletal branches covered in snow. I listen out for another scream, but the icy silence permeates my fur and fills my gut with cold dread.

Shuddering, I lean down to the side and scan my surroundings for signs of Natalia. At the bottom of the garden stands what looks like a dilapidated shed, but no snowflakes cling to its roof.

"Over there."

Bardolph tips his antlers, taking us to the shed in two powerful strides. He stops outside, pawing at the ground with a hoof, his eyes trained on the door. A loud crash pierces the air from inside, making Bardolph lurch forward.

"No."

Not wanting Natalia hurt by bursting through the structure on my moose, I leap off his back and race toward the door.

Deep male laughter grates across my eardrums, powering my steps. I pull back my fist, gather my strength, and shatter the door with one punch.

I see the wizard first holding aloft a six-foot-long staff that shoots red magic to a bundle curled up in the corner.

It's my beautiful Natalia.

And she's hurt.

Chapter Nine

NATALIA

One minute, I'm about to get fucked by the Krampus and his huge cock, then the next, I'm flying backward through my own chimney.

My stomach lurches as the magic propels me through the sooty chute. I squeeze my eyes shut, hold my breath, and try to stretch out my arms to stop the enchantment, but a blast of power wraps them back around my chest.

Shit.

A tiny part of me knew it was too good to be true.

Every year, I send a message to Father Christmas to give me a man worth fucking. The moment I get a taste of his delicious dick, some force of magic pulls us apart.

Or maybe this was all just a big trick.

Krampus said I was on his naughty list, right? Maybe the BDSM was a test to see if I could take a birching without begging for sex. Maybe I liked it too much, and the magic of Christmas is sending me to hell.

My heart kicks up a notch.

Oh fuck.

I don't want to die.

Cold air blasts on my face, pulling me out of my panic, and a second later, I'm thrown onto something hard and splintery.

"Shit!"

I crack open an eye, scramble to my feet, and find myself no longer inside the chimney but in a wooden structure the size of a shed.

Moonlight streams in through the gaps in the wood-work, bringing gusts of icy wind that mingle with the mold and decay. It also reminds me I'm not wearing a skirt.

Or knickers.

"Where the fuck is this?"

I clap a hand over my crotch and head toward the door. Unless this is a special part of the afterlife reserved for hot-blooded witches, I seriously doubt that I'm in hell.

The door wings open, and a large figure steps inside, wearing a black cloak.

I really want to adopt a more assertive stance—hands on hips, shoulders back, thrusted-out chest—but that would be awkward with the lack of a skirt and knickers.

"W-who are you?" I ask, trying to keep the tremble from my voice. "You can't touch me, I'm protected by a guild."

"You used me for free drinks," says a familiar voice. "You laughed in my face, you belittled my cock and ignored my final demand."

My brows pull together. Don't tell me it's the dick-fishing guy I met online?

"Stan?" I ask.

He pulls off his hood, revealing the blond man from earlier, his features twisted into a rictus of fury. Stan lifts a long staff, sending a beam of red magic into my chest.

Fire burns through my insides, making me drop to my hands and knees.

"I'm sick of you bitches," Stan yells. "Making sexy promises, getting a guy turned on, then kicking him out."

"But you lied," I say through clenched teeth.

Another blast of magic has me screaming, drowning out his barrage of insults. I'm in so much trouble. Krampus won't know where I've gone and will probably think I tricked him and left.

Without a phone or a wand, I've got no chance of escaping. I curl up into a tight ball, protecting my insides. In a minute, Stan will stop for another rant or to boast. That will give me the chance to catch my breath and attack. Then I'll use his phone to call the enforcers, and he'll spend the next ten years in jail.

The pain intensifies, searing through my veins like molten lightning. I cry out, my breath smelling of burned flesh and blood. I'm not sure how much more of this I can take.

Moments later, a loud crash shakes the floors, bringing in a blast of cold air, and an end to Stan's painful magic.

"Who are you?" Stans yells, his voice rising several octaves. "What are you doing?"

Relief floods my system, and I slump on the floor, panting hard. Maybe someone heard the screaming and called the enforcers? I need to send a message to Krampus. He has to know he wasn't ghosted.

"Natalia Jasper belongs to me," bellows another familiar voice.

My head snaps up.

The huge bulk of the Krampus fills the doorway. Snowflakes sizzle on the ends of his fur as though he's on fire. He's so tall that he needs to dip his head to enter and so broad that he needs to turn his body to the side.

Stan skitters backward, holding his staff in front of him like a shield. "You can't come in here."

The Krampus turns to me, his amber irises burning with fury. They dim as our gazes meet, and his brows pull together with concern.

My chest constricts. He must have come looking for me. I swallow hard and give him a nod and a tiny smile to let him know I'm not hurt.

The tightness in his features loosens, as though he's relieved I'm alright. I have to blink a few times to process what I'm seeing. Most guys would be outraged that Stan interrupted his sexcapade, but Krampus really seems to care. His eyes soften for a moment before he turns his attention toward the man screaming in front of me.

"Bastard." Krampus raises a clawed hand toward Stan, but it's his chains that wrap around Stan's neck and hurls him to the side.

Stan screams and hits the wall and lands on his staff, breaking it into two.

"You touched what belongs to the Krampus!" he roars.

"Wait." Stan raises his palms. "If it's about the girl, take her. Natalia means nothing to me—"

"Stanley Baxter Arius, aged thirty-four years, four months, and twelve days. Do not speak her name," the Krampus yells.

"How do you know—" Stan makes a choking sound. "Oh, shit. You really exist."

I sit up, my heart pounding hard enough to drown out Stan's pleading. No one has ever rushed to my defense. Not unless it was part of their job. The Krampus has only known me for a few minutes, and he hasn't even finished punishing the wicked, yet he's ready to spend Christmas Eve offering me protection.

Tears sting the backs of my eyes. I've never felt safer.

"Krampus," I whisper, my voice broken.

He looks at me, the anger in his expression fading into

something gentle and possessive. Each step he takes toward me makes my heart soar. His gaze drops to my bare legs and travels up to my exposed pussy.

"Close your wretched eyes, boy." He bares his teeth and snarls at Stan, who whimpers.

Krampus softens his gaze and offers me his hand. "Natalia, are you alright?"

I let him help me to my feet. "Fine. Just a bit of bruising to my ego."

His nostrils flare, presumably at the thought of any part of me being bruised by someone other than him, but he tucks me into his side.

Warmth soaks into my flesh as his shaggy pelt wraps around my body like a fur coat. Gazing up into his amber eyes, I offer him a relieved smile.

In an unusually gentle voice, he says, "I already know the answer to this question, but for the sake of formality, I must ask."

I melt against his strong body. "What?"

"Who did this to you?" the Krampus roars.

Stan screams.

Okay, this is odd. Krampus caught Stan in the act of torturing me half to death and even stopped him, so he already knows who put me in this state. But then again, who am I to question the ways of ancient gods?

"He did." I point at Stan.

"Wait." Stan scrambles to his feet. "If you're doing what I think you're about to do—"

"Silence," the Krampus bellows. "You touched what is mine, defiled and gazed upon her naked body."

"She was like that when I found her," Stan screams.

"And you subjected her to the most heinous of spells. Stanley Baxter Arius, you have been a very naughty boy, and by the power vested in me by Christmas, I cast you into hell."

The Krampus punches the air with one mighty fist, shattering the fabric of reality. Smoke and flames and the scent of sulfur bursts out from a tiny portal that expands to the width of the door.

Now, it's my turn to scream, "Is that hell?"

The Krampus gives me a gentle squeeze. "This naughty boy touched you. No amount of birching will rectify that affront."

"Right," I rasp.

Stan turns to me, his gaze pleading.

"Nat, please don't let him do this to me. I don't deserve eternal punishment."

Some women might plead on Stanley's behalf and say that he should get another chance. Not me. What kind of man catfishes women with fake dick pics and then becomes murderous when they refuse to pay his expenses or suck his cock?

How many other women has he victimized? How far would he have gone today if he hadn't been stopped?

Stan is a fucking menace.

I fold my arms across my chest. "Go to hell."

The portal swallows him up and engulfs him with flames. My breath turns shallow, and I sway on my feet, but Krampus holds me steady.

"Forgive me," he says.

I turn to meet amber eyes brimming with sorrow. "What are you talking about?"

"You got hurt."

"But that's not your fault."

The Krampus winces. "You were under the care of a god. All you should have felt was comfort and pleasure."

"There's nothing to forgive." I place a hand on his furry pectoral muscle. "No one has ever fought my battles."

His chest heaves, and my palm vibrates with his rumbling growl. "Not enough."

"What do you mean?"

"I want more names."

I rear back. "Eh?"

"Tell me every man who has ever touched your delicate flesh," he snarls. "I will cast them all to hell."

Chapter Ten

NATALIA

I can't tell which burns brighter—the fury in the eyes of the Krampus or the fires of hell. Call me heartless, but Stan deserved what he got. That entitled prick was a walking red flag with an arsenal of dangerous magic. Worst combination ever.

But my exes?

A shiver runs down my spine at the prospect of banishing them into a dimension of eternal torment. Not all of them were bad.

"Do not keep me waiting," Krampus snarls.

My throat constricts, and it's not just because of the overwhelming stench of hell. I run my fingers down Krampus's furry chest, eliciting a shiver.

"Krampus—"

"I like it when you call me by name," he rumbles.

"Why do you want to hurt all these men?"

"You're mine," he says. "Any man who has come before me must perish."

So, he's possessive.

I clear my throat. To be honest, I thought this would be a one-night stand, and the Krampus would disappear to Lapland or wherever. Any deity so generously endowed must have a harem of willing sex kittens.

"About that... What are we?"

His eyes narrow. "You are mine. I'm claiming you."

I freeze. Claiming me? "Like the way a Dom might claim his submissive?"

"If that's the way you want to see it, yes, since you're about to become mine." Krampus tilts my chin up with a clawed finger and growls, "Do you accept?"

My mouth goes dry. It's like he can see right through me. He wants something deeper than a casual fling, something I've always wanted, but why does that scare me more than facing down a horde of sexually disgruntled wizards?

I gaze into his amber eyes, my heart fluttering like the wings of the fairy on my Christmas tree. "But what about my job? I can't move to the North Pole."

Pain flashes in his eyes, and he jerks his head to the side.

Wait—did I hurt him?

Words spill from my lips faster than I can stop them. "I'm not rejecting you, I promise, but I've spent ages training to become a tech witch, and I just finished decorating my first apartment. There's no way I can give up the life I have here. Is there a way we can make this work?"

His expression softens, revealing a vulnerable soul beneath his grumpy exterior. When he cups my cheek, my heart swells.

"I would never take you from your job." He pulls back and swipes a claw over my cheekbone. "But there are ways we can be together."

"How?"

"When you're not busy with your duties, we'll make it work."

"Thank you," I whisper.

He presses his mouth to my forehead. "Don't thank me until after your punishment."

My jaw drops. "What?"

"Is that any way to speak to your Dom?"

"Sorry, sir!" I squeeze my thighs together at the prospect of getting chastised as a brat. "But why the punishment?"

"Abandonment during sexual discourse, refusal to supply the names of the men who touched you, allowing that wretched creature to see your beautiful cunt." He sits on the floor and pulls me across his lap.

I yelp, my arms and legs flailing, but he presses a large hand over my shoulder blades and keeps me in place.

"Your sentence is to receive two spankings for each man."

Arousal sparks between my legs as I struggle within his tight grip. I've never been spanked before. All the corporal punishment I received at the foster home was magical.

A cool draft wafts across the room, tickling my exposed ass cheeks. I squirm against the matted fur and groan. There isn't enough time for my skin to tighten into goosebumps, because the next thing I feel is heat.

Slap!

His palm strikes my ass with a sting that travels down my pussy, gathers in my clit, and sizzles like static.

I arch my back and cry out.

"Count the spanks."

"One."

The pain fades, and he gives my sore cheek a slow, sensual stroke. Moisture pools in my core as he rubs gentle circles over my sore flesh, and I relax my thighs. One of his fingers travels so close to my pussy that I groan.

Fuck, this feels so good.

Slap!

I squeeze my eyes shut and bite down on my bottom lip. It's silly to be so shocked. I knew there would be more, but I'd gotten so used to the pleasure. Now, the second spank is so sharp and sudden, it feels as though I'm being licked by a hot flame.

"Two."

My muscles clench, only to relax again with his soothing caresses. This time, I part my legs even further, so he can see exactly what he does to me. If I'm lucky, he might fill me with one of those thick fingers.

"Are you wet for me?" he asks.

"Always," I whisper.

Slap!

"Three," I moan.

As he massages my ass this time, one of his fingers skims my pussy lips, infusing me with a thrill of arousal. I tilt my hips, exposing more of my sex, but he pulls his hand away, ready for another slap.

"You're doing this so I don't build up a tolerance," I say, my words slurring.

"I'm doing this because you're a naughty girl who likes having her pussy spanked."

"What?"

His palm lands on my sex, causing my inner walls to flex and clench.

My hands fly to my face, and I let out a long, throaty groan. "Oh fuck... That's four."

He runs a possessive hand down my back, and I close my eyes, allowing myself to melt into surrender. My mind is a haze, my body a furnace. This feels so right, and I've never felt so complete. The spanking continues, alternating between pleasure and delicious pain.

I'm not sure how long it will continue since I've had sex

with six guys but have allowed myself to be touched by more.

Heat builds up on each ass cheek that spreads to my hungry core. I buck my hips in time with his practiced hand, wanting more, needing at least a finger—better still, his cock. Every third spank he delivers goes directly on my needy, clenching pussy.

"Twelve," I say, my voice hoarse.

He drags his hand away, leaving me a trembling, panting mess. My ass is still stinging from the spanks, but my core is burning for more.

"Please." The word comes out as a whisper.

"Tell me, Natalia. Use your words."

"Cock."

He chuckles and pulls me closer, letting me feel the huge bulge trapped beneath his fur. "This?"

"Fuck me, please."

"You don't know what you're asking for," he says, sounding solemn.

His chest rises and falls like bellows, and his features tighten. Maybe he's never had sex before or he's worried about stretching me too far. Maybe he's just nervous about taking this step and wants to know I'm sure.

Looking him deep in the eyes, I infuse my voice with all my sincerity. "I do," I murmur. "Nothing would satisfy me more."

He cocks his head to the side. "Truly?"

"I need it. I need you."

"Beg, and I will fuck you with my tongue. If you can handle its girth, then I may gift you with my cock."

"Please, let me have you, Sir. Deep inside me."

"I'm listening," he rumbles.

"Please, Sir. Fill me up."

My words elicit a satisfied growl that I feel all along the length of my body.

"Give me those names," he says.

I bite down on my bottom lip. Krampus stopped spanking me at twelve, so he knows more about me than appears. It seems disloyal, but I can't in good conscience allow innocent men to die.

"Not all of them," I say. "Just the bastards who hurt me."

"Fine," he snarls and pulls me upright.

Blood rushes to my head, filling my vision with spots. As Krampus adjusts me to face him and straddle his lap, I blink away the dots.

We're no longer in the wooden room. We're no longer in any kind of structure. The ground is black and covered with a thin layer of ash. Every few feet, it splits, revealing molten-orange lava.

But that's not the most disturbing part.

Tall boulders surround us, which both hold back what looks like a wall of flames and muffle the echo of tortured screams. Beyond the boulders stand tall mountains coughing smoke and spewing liquid fire.

I grab handfuls of his fur and whisper, "Is this hell?"

"You deserve a change of scenery." He rolls out a long, red tongue that's as broad and as thick as my palm. "By the time I've finished fucking you with my tongue, every man who ever caused you pain will burn."

Chapter Eleven

NATALIA

I'm so wet and needy that out surroundings no longer matter. My pussy clenches around nothing, needing to be filled with anything—fingers, cock, or tongue, as long as I get to cum.

Krampus lays me out on a warm stone bed and pulls my legs so far apart that my thighs ache. A warm breeze wafts in through the tall boulder, hitting my swollen clit.

I arch my back and moan, "Hurry."

He positions himself between my spread legs, his huge tongue lolling to the side. "Are you going to be a good girl for the Krampus or an impatient one?"

"Sorry sir," I say with a whimper.

His amber eyes drift down from my mouth and over my clothed upper half. I don't know if it's because he's a god or we're in hell, but his lingering gaze feels like a caress.

"You are wearing too many clothes," he growls.

"I-I can take them off," I reply.

"No need."

He leans down, letting his tongue snake up my inner

thigh, detonating tiny bursts of pleasure across my nerves. I curl my toes and shiver at the prospect of him reaching my clit.

The tongue slows as he reaches the outer lips of my pussy, and makes the barest contact with my pubes. My body quivers, needing more.

"Please," I whisper.

"You will be silent and take what you're given," he growls.

I clench my teeth and bite back a complaint. Krampus is a control freak, but it's kind of nice to have a man in charge who wants to take his time.

"Yes, sir," I say.

He gives my thigh a gentle squeeze. "Good girl."

When the tongue wanders up my hip, I squeeze my eyes shut and groan. He licks a path over my belly, beneath my blouse, and under my bra.

Then his tongue splits into two and rolls my nipple.

Pleasure shoots straight to my clit, making my hips rise off the stone platform. "Oh, fuck."

"Easy now," Krampus says with a dark chuckle. "Once I've finished priming these juicy nipples, I'm going to do the same to your clit."

My clit pulses. Without meaning to, I bring my thighs together to create a little friction.

"Keep those legs open," he barks. "I want full access to that pretty wet cunt."

With a moan, I spread my thighs, letting in a breeze. The air in hell is soupy and thick, so each draft feels like I'm being fondled by ghostly fingers.

As Krampus continues massaging my nipples with his forked tongue, invisible hands unfasten the buttons of my blouse.

"What's happening?" I ask.

"Open your eyes," he rumbles.

I crack open an eye to find long strands of fur branching off his body like vines. My mouth drops open. Some of the strands have wrapped around my wrists, others around my ankles and thighs, but the majority are unfastening what's left of my clothes.

"What else can you do with that fur?" I ask.

"Spread you open while I feast," he replies with a broad grin.

Now that I'm naked, he releases my nipple, only for the strands of fur to take their place. It's softer than I imagined and wraps around each peak like twine.

The Krampus licks a wet path between my breasts, trailing warm saliva that sends a rush of arousal straight to my pussy.

"You like being teased," he says.

I shake my head.

"Liar."

His tongue makes painful flicks against my clit, creating sparks of delicious pain. On instinct, my thighs pull together, but his fur holds them in place.

Bondage via Krampus fur?

Kinky.

He delivers another tongue flick on my clit's sensitive underside, making the muscles of my pussy clench.

"Okay," I say through panting breaths. "I like being teased. I love it when you make me wait."

His deep rumbling chuckle tickles my nerves, infusing me with an odd sense of comfort and safety. "Good little witches get rewards."

Before I can ask what he'll do next, the tongue slides between my folds. The tip of his tongue pushes into my opening, stretching it wide. I suck in a deep breath, preparing for him to stroke my g-spot again, but all I feel is an immense fullness.

Tongues are nothing like cocks. While erections are hard and unmovable, tongues are infinitely more flexible. This particular one is covered in thick taste buds that drag up and down my inner walls.

The tongue reaches my cervix and expands. My muscles flutter around it, needing friction, and I try to buck my hips.

"Stay still," he growls. "You'll need a good stretching if you're going to survive my cock."

"A-alright."

He takes a deep breath, puffs out his huge chest, and looms over me like a specter. The fiery flecks in his eyes turn red as he exhales, and the tongue in my pussy inflates.

Shivers dance down the length of my spine. I've never felt so full, so filled, so fulfilled. And this is all without an orgasm.

"So big," I moan.

"It's for your own good," he says with a groan. "I need you nice and limber for a hard fucking."

The tongue stretching my pussy is now thicker than a standard wine bottle and only getting larger. It twitches inside me, making the thick tastebuds stroke up and down my walls.

The fleshy little protrusions reach my g-spot, each caress pushing me to a higher level of arousal. The sensation builds and builds until I'm panting with desire, my hips rocking and my clit throbbing.

"Please," I say, my voice broken.

"Not yet."

His tongue expands even further, pushing against my organs until I can barely breathe.

"Don't," I whisper. "You're pressing my bladder."

"Then you will squirt."

I shake my head. "Keep doing that, and I will pee."

The Krampus chuckles, the sound low and rich. "Let it all out. I can take it."

The pressure intensifies, and I clench every muscle, trying to keep in the waterworks. There's no way I can piss over anyone, let alone a god, let alone in hell. What if he gets offended and decides to leave me here to the creatures screeching behind those walls?

"Natalia." His sharp voice cuts through my fretting. "You are holding back."

"For your own good," I say between clenched teeth.

"Let's see how well you hold up when my tongue inflates again."

He sucks in another deep breath, his chest expanding even broader than it did before. I tense my muscles, determined not to pee.

With another exhale, he expands his tongue, this time to twice its girth. I'm panting hard. It's too much—the impossible stretch, the taste buds tormenting my g-spot, the extra pressure on my bladder.

"You are a stubborn little witch," Krampus says.

"I'd like to exercise my safe word," I mutter.

He throws his head back and laughs. "There are no safe words in hell."

My muscles tremble around his tongue, and my clit throbs to the rapid beat of my pulse. I'm dangerously close to losing control and climaxing all over Krampus. Who knows what my body will eject?

I can't let loose and spray him.

"If you really want me to stop, I will," he says, sounding serious.

"N-no," I groan. "But don't punish me if I make a mess."

"I will punish my little witch as I see fit," he roars.

I slump down on the rock and groan. He's never going

to let me win. If the Krampus is going to get angry, then I may as well get my orgasm.

"Alright then," I murmur. "Do your worst."

A strand of fur coils around my clit and then makes up-and-down motions like a pump. The tongue that's stretching me to the point of insanity moves back and forth, letting each thick tastebud drag along my inner walls.

As the strands of fur tighten around my nipples, I close my eyes and surrender to the sensations.

"Eyes on me."

I force my eyes open, finding the Krampus hovering so close that I feel the crackle of his fur against my skin. His eyes are so bright that it feels like I'm looking into the flames.

"Good girl," he says, his voice hoarse. "Now, I want you to cum."

Chapter Twelve

NATALIA

Pressure builds up around my clit, making it throb harder than my racing heartbeat. I writhe beneath the Krampus as far as my restraints will allow, each brush of his fur against my skin infusing me with tiny sparks of pleasure.

The thick tongue stretching me open pulls in and out of my pussy, pushing me to a delicious edge.

I clench my teeth, shake my head from side to side, and moan. Every inch of my body screams for release. I can't hold back.

But I must.

"Naughty girl," he rumbles in my ear. "Wring my tongue with that tight little cunt, drench me with your juices. If you don't I will spank your ass so raw you'll be feeling it until next Christmas!"

My clit swells even further at the promise of another punishment, and a strand of fur lashes at it with a tiny crack.

I come apart. All the pressure, all the pleasure, all the little pulsations that built up during the time I've spent in hell release with a noisy scream.

Warm liquid shoots from the little hole beneath my clit, soaking Krampus's fur. Any other time, I might cringe and stiffen, but this orgasm is all-consuming.

"Good girl. You're doing so well."

His praise sends my head into a tailspin, and it feels like the smoke and flames and steam form a vortex around our clearing.

My inner walls release and clench, infusing me with a burst of euphoria that I feel from my scalp to the tips of my toes. It's like surfing a cyclone or riding a broomstick in a thunderstorm.

"Fuck, Natalia," Krampus groans. "I love the way you pulse around my tongue."

My legs tremble within their restraints, and I pull at my wrists, wanting to wrap my arms around Krampus and offer him my eternal devotion. I gaze into his eyes, beyond the flames, seeing admiration, love, and centuries of loneliness that surpass mine.

"Krampus..." My voice breaks.

How can someone so good at sex ever be alone?

"Shhh..." He wraps his arms around my back and cradles me to his chest. "I know."

I groan at the broken connection, but it's replaced by the comfort of his larger body. Then another wave of pleasure knocks me to one side, and my eyes roll to the back of my head.

As the climax fades, relaxation sweeps through my system, and every muscle in my body goes limp. I have never cum so long or hard—not with my magic-operated toys, not with my tentacle grinders, not with the illegal crystal dildos I once bought from a coven of man-hating witches.

This is utterly sublime.

He pulls out his tongue, bringing me back to harsh reality.

"Please stay," I say, my voice breathy.

Krampus draws back, meeting my gaze with twinkling eyes. "You said you wanted my cock."

"I do."

"Now that I've stretched you out, you should be able to handle my girth. Are you ready for it, Natalia?"

I bite my lip, feeling like I've already had a Christmas present to make up for every small dick, and cheating asshole I've had to endure. But I'll never say no to more.

"Please," I say. "Fill me up."

The restraints on my arms and legs loosen, then Krampus rises and offers me his hand.

I glance around the clearing. "What's wrong with doing it over here?"

He pulls me off the platform and into his arms. "Names."

It takes a moment to register that he wants the names of my exes. "Are you going to kill them?"

"Do you have a problem with that?"

"No."

"Then we will begin."

The platform morphs into a stone throne, and Krampus sits down and settles me onto his lap. Strands of fur wrap around my crotch and breasts, forming a hairy bikini.

He snaps a finger, and an eight-foot-tall demon with red skin appears, holding a man by the scruff of the neck. A black leather hood covers his head, but from the slight paunch and the familiar shape of his dick, I can already tell it's Stan the dickfisher.

My brow rises. "Who's that other guy?"

"Dark elf," Krampus mutters. "I have eight of them at my command, and they mostly reside in hell."

The dark elf tears off Stan's gimp mask.

"Nat!" Stan flails his arms. "What are you doing here? Help me."

"Like you did when you stole me from my home and put me under those curses?" I curl my lip, lean back into the comfort of my new Dom, and wait for the show.

Stan whines. "That's different—"

"Silence," Krampus roars. He places a hand on my thigh. "Natalia, give me the first name, and one of my dark elves will deliver him to your feet."

My mind conjures up the image of the man who took my virginity, subjected me to orgasmless sex, and then cheated.

"Richard Biggins," I say, my hands curling into fists.

Another dark elf materializes, holding a man dressed like Father Christmas. The fake beard bursts into flames, revealing a soot-covered Richard.

"What's happening." Richard glances around, his gaze falling on me. "Hey, don't I know you?"

Heat flares across my cheeks. "Forgotten me already? It's Natalia Jasper from the guild."

Richard gives me a blank look, reminding me of how insignificant I felt that time I caught him cheating with another guild member. I sit straighter on my Dom's lap, feeling a surge of power.

I, Natalia Jasper, managed to ensnare an old god. Richard Biggins is a worm.

The Krampus gets me to summon a few more: the next guy who dated me to steal my magic, and the other who ran up a boatload of debts. I won't mention any of the one-night stands because those were brief encounters purely for sex.

"That's all?" Krampus asks.

"They're the ones that matter."

He hesitates, and I hold my breath, hoping he doesn't demand the names of the other guys.

"Very good," Krampus says with a grunt. "How do you want them to suffer, Natalia?"

I lean back against his broad chest and luxuriate in the thick fur. "They no longer matter to me. I already have the perfect man."

"Now, now," Krampus says with a deep chuckle.

"Nat," Stanley cries. "Help me."

"Cut off Stan's cock and balls, roast them over the fires of hell, and serve them with a ketchup made of his blood," I say with a shrug. "The others get to stay and watch."

"Anything else?" he asks.

"While Stan's enjoying their meal let them all feel every ounce of pain they inflicted on me."

"Excellent." Krampus snaps his fingers, summoning another quartet of elves. "Make sure these wretched humans suffer the prescribed punishments."

All four of the men scream out for me, including Richard, who has either remembered my name or gotten his cue from the others.

"Are you ready to go home?" the Krampus murmurs.

My stomach tightens with a touch of trepidation. Tonight has been so exhilarating, and not just the carnage on my exes or even the mind-blowing sex. There was a moment of connection when he was stretching my pussy with his tongue when I thought he felt the same raw need for companionship. Maybe I was mistaken?

I twist around on his lap, trying to meet his gaze. "Are we parting ways already?"

He lowers his eyes and sighs. I pull my brows together, wondering why he's hesitating.

"I thought you might want breakfast after we fuck," he mutters.

The air fills with screams, but my chest fills with warmth. My heart makes an excited flutter. I would follow the Krampus anywhere, even if he sleeps on a bed of furs within an icy cave.

"I'd love to spend Christmas morning with you," I murmur.

He gathers me into his arms again and rises from his throne, leaving behind the elves torturing my exes. Waving a hand through the air, he creates a portal into a cozy bedroom of wood-paneled walls illuminated by a roaring fire.

"Come, Little Witch," he says and steps through the portal. "Let's get you some cock."

Chapter Thirteen

KRAMPUS

I cannot in good conscience have my first time with Natalia in hell. Hell is no place for the woman I've come to respect. Natalia never once recoiled from my monstrous appearance, didn't so much as flinch at the prospect of punishing her former lovers for eternity.

Her beauty, her bravery, and her acceptance have captured my heart.

The only reason I brought her there was to buy time for the dark elves to prepare my bedroom. After decades in that dungeon, I expect Klaus has let my chambers fall to ruin.

Sending Bardolph a silent apology for abandoning him on Christmas Eve, I step through the portal into my home.

My minions have made some upgrades to the previous decor. The wood shingle is now panels of polished pinewood, with velvet tapestries depicting scenes of me flying through the skies with my moose.

They have lined one wall with the kind of leather-bound books my brother enjoys and provided furniture crafted from the finest pine wood, including a four-poster bed adorned with a white satin canopy and drapes.

Natalia's breath catches. "You live here? This is wonderful."

I hesitate, wondering if I should tell her the ugly truth about my confinement. She has been so open with me, I can't help but want to be honest with her in return.

"This was once my home." I gesture at the walls. "But for the past nine decades, I have lived in a dungeon."

"Where, how?"

"I was imprisoned beneath this house."

Natalia brushes her fingers along my arm, infusing my heart with an unfamiliar warmth. "Who did that to you?"

"My brother," I growl.

"Why?"

My jaw clenches. The last thing I want to talk about is him, but I manage to grind out, "He wants everything that's good, including the spirit of Christmas!"

"Will he continue to be a problem?" she asks, her brows gathering into a frown.

I shake my head. "No. I won't allow it. Besides, he already admitted that he was wrong to lock me up. He will no longer interfere with my Christmas duties."

Natalia gazes into my eyes, and the hand on my arm slides up to my jaw. "I'm sorry you had to endure a fate like that. But I'm glad you're home."

"Do you like it?"

"It's perfect," she whispers and gestures to a pine wood stand beside the bed holding leather paddles, floggers, and canes. "Can we play a little after we've fucked? You've even got us a rack of toys."

Us.

Her words bring a lump to my throat. I have never been

with a woman long enough for there to be an 'us,' yet here she is, embracing the fact that we have a future.

Swallowing hard, I press a gentle kiss on her forehead. "Thank you, Little Witch."

I carry her across the room, passing a Saint Andrew's cross and a spanking bench, and close the portal to hell. The screaming stops, leaving the chamber silent, save for the snap and crackle of the fireplace.

Natalia slips her hand down my chest and over my abs. "I'm not sure how long I can wait to feel you inside me."

My cock hardens. This time, I allow it to escape its sheath. I open the silky bed curtains, lay Natalia down on the furry coverlet, and spread apart her thighs.

Natalia peers up at me through half-lidded eyes, her cheeks flushed, and her full lips parted. Her gaze travels down my body, landing on the erection pointing toward her, and she parts her thighs to reveal her obscenely wet pussy.

She is the very vision of loveliness, and she's all mine.

"Look at you," I say. "So eager for my cock."

She stretches out her arms and whimpers, "Please."

"I'm going to enter you nice and slow, and you will feel every inch. We're alone right now, so nobody will hear you scream."

Natalia licks her lips.

My heart pounds harder than it did when I escaped from prison. I'm almost certain that stretching Natalia with my tongue will prepare her for my girth, but if I tear her apart—

I cut off that thought. Natalia is a witch, not a human sacrifice. She is strong. My head is clear, I won't fall into a frenzy, but I'm not going to ruin someone so precious.

"Get on top," I snarl.

Her jaw drops. "What?"

"You said you wanted my cock? Then take it. Ride me hard and fast. Ride me to my satisfaction or you will be spanked."

Natalia's breath quickens, and she scrambles to her knees. "Yes, sir!"

I lower myself onto the bed, resting my palms behind me on the mattress. "Show me what you've got, Little Witch."

She straddles me, her hands on my shoulders, her knees on either side of my hips. I grab my cock by the base and tilt it backward, so the head is level with her pussy.

"Take your time," I say.

"A-alright."

Balling my free hand into a fist, I force myself to stay still. Witch or not, Natalia has entrusted me with her body. We will fuck at a pace that's safe for her.

Natalia will not die like the others.

Chapter Fourteen

NATALIA

My legs tremble as Krampus's cockhead nudges against my entrance. The intensity of his gaze makes my pulse quicken. He could take what he wants from me with a single thrust, but he's allowing me to set the pace... At least for the first time.

I'd better make this good because men like the Krampus have high expectations.

With a deep breath, I lower myself onto his cock, feeling the incredible strain. His girth stretches me, pushing me to my limit, but every nerve ending lights up like sparklers on a yule log.

I bite down on my bottom lip. This is more than I've ever handled. "Oh, fuck."

The Krampus lets out a low growl and places a hand on my hip. "Are you alright?"

"This is incredible," I say, my voice breathy.

His face softens, and he gives me an encouraging nod. "You look so beautiful, sliding down my cock and squeezing its head with your tight little pussy."

"Yes, sir."

"Now, ride me, little witch."

I slide down, taking him inch by delicious inch. Even though I'm already relaxed from his huge tongue, it's a completely different experience with his cock.

For starters, I've never had one that's L-shaped, let alone with such a huge, bulbous tip. It's like a Christmas Stocking stuffed full of meat.

My walls hug and squeeze his length as I descend, making him moan and pant. Knowing that I'm having such an effect on a god makes my nipples tighten, and my pussy even slicker.

He grunts, looking like he's trying hard not to thrust.

I can understand why.

His cock bends at an angle several inches below the tip, where it expands to nearly twice its girth and stretches my entrance to the point of aching. The mix of pain and pleasure makes every nerve in my body thrum.

It's too much—I'm so stuffed. The blunt cockhead presses on my cervix and the thick veins and ridges drag against the walls. Every inch of his shaft fills my pussy, yet my body aches for more.

"Yes, just like that," he murmurs. "You're fucking me so well."

"I-I can't take any more," I groan. "You're too fucking big."

"Take it slow and steady this first time," he says. "Enjoy the ride. The next, I will make you take it all."

At his words, my arousal surges, and I push down, engulfing more of his girth. He grabs my hips, guiding me to rise toward his thick cockhead.

Gasping, I cling onto his broad shoulders and rotate my hips, so my clit brushes against his thick fur. My toes curl and my breath comes in ragged pants as I build up a steady rhythm.

"Such a good little witch," he rumbles. "Taking my cock like you were made for it."

His guttural groans echo in my ears, fanning the flames of my desire. I'm his slut, his toy, his little witch, and I'm loving every second of it.

My eyelids flutter shut as I lose myself in the sensations. It's more exhilarating than the first time I produced electricity with a wand or the time I drank a potion that made me float.

"Look at me, Natalia," he says. "I want to see you come apart around my cock."

My gaze snaps up to meet his, and what I see in his eyes makes my breath catch. Deep within the flames is a reflection of myself but through some kind of beauty filter.

The version looking back at me has fuller lips, perfectly thick and tousled mahogany hair, and the kind of curvaceous body witches can only achieve with corsets. I grip the fur on his shoulders, my mouth falling open. Is that how Krampus sees me? Some kind of wild, desirable creature?

Just when I'm losing myself in this mirrored version of myself, Krampus moves one of his hands up to my breast, kneading and stroking it until I'm panting and losing my rhythm.

My pulse quickens, and I ride him harder, faster, my entire body quivering like a wand during a powerful spell. I'm so close—

"You're mine, little witch," he growls.

"Yours."

"I'm going to fill you up, and you'll take every drop."

"A-aah!"

"So fucking tight."

"Yes."

The pressure builds until I can barely take it. I'm so overwhelmed with sensations that my head spins. Krampus continues his filthy tirade with words that fuel my arousal until I can barely concentrate on riding his cock.

"Come for me, little witch," he says, his voice a deep command that pushes me closer and closer to the edge.

"Now," he roars.

My release hits me like a backfiring spell, and euphoria splinters me into a million pieces. I cry out, my pussy quivering and clenching around his impossible girth. My vision blurs, and I lose myself in the intensity of the climax.

His muscles tighten, looking like he's close to cumming. He grabs my hips with both hands with a roar that makes my skin tremble.

Hot liquid floods my depths, pushing my orgasm to new heights. His eyes roll back, and he drops his head forward, panting. I collapse onto his broad chest, still shaking with the aftershocks.

"You were perfect, little witch," he says, his voice laced with desire. "If only I had someone like you while I was in captivity. I would never have left."

I pull back to meet his bright amber eyes, remembering what he'd said earlier. "What happened?"

"My brother fought me over the punishment of bad children, and that fight turned into a bloody battle."

I rest my head on his broad chest, picturing two horned gods tearing at each other with claws. "Aren't siblings supposed to get over their rivalries at this age?"

Krampus chuckles. "Do you not have a brother or sister?"

"I grew up in foster homes. Most people didn't stick around to form bonds," I mumble.

"That must have been lonely." He runs his clawed fingers

through my hair. "I've always had my brother, no matter how much we fought."

I dip my head. "It wasn't so bad. At least I knew I could leave as soon as I turned eighteen. Then I'd be free to fall in love, start a family, and give myself all the things I ever wanted."

A low growl builds up in his chest, making my head snap up to meet his amber eyes. "What's wrong?"

"When I think of you betrayed by those men, I want to kill them all over again."

My heart flutters, and I wrap my arms around his massive neck. "No one has ever protected me. Thank you, Krampus."

"You're my little witch," he whispers. "I will fight for your honor until the end of time, and protect you with my dying breath. The only male who will ever touch you again is me."

A lump forms in my throat, and I swallow. Wizards will say anything to get into a witch's pants, only to change their minds once they've cum. But the Krampus wants more. From the sounds of things, he's serious about giving me a future. Everything about the way he speaks and acts tells me that he's trustworthy.

The tight band of anxiety I've held around my chest loosens at the thought that I finally have someone who wants me as much as I want him.

"Really?" I ask, the backs of my eyes stinging with happy tears.

He wraps his arms around my waist and pulls me close, his body forming a furry cocoon around mine. Krampus hasn't just filled my pussy—he's filled my heart.

My muscles clench around his softening cock, which is still deliciously thick. His response is to squeeze me tighter and groan.

"I could stay inside your sweet cunt forever," he says with a deep growl. "You don't ever have to worry about being alone."

He's given me something I never had—the security of knowing someone will always stand by my side, no matter what.

I'm no longer alone.

"Thank you," I whisper, my voice choked. "And if at any point you get locked up again, I'll find a way to join you in prison."

He makes a rumbling laugh. "Thanks to you, I forgot about punishing children this year. My brother will be pleased."

"Glad I could keep you distracted," I say.

Before he can form an answer, a huge bang makes the entire room tremble.

I stiffen in his embrace. "What's happening?"

The Krampus growls. "Bardolph, settle down."

"Who's that?" I ask.

"My moose," he grumbles. "He's furious because I left him in the human world."

An even louder bang sends dust falling from the ceiling. I wince. "Maybe he's anxious and thinking your brother locked you up again."

"You could be right," Krampus mumbles and tilts forward, depositing me on the bed.

"Are you leaving?" I clutch at his fur.

"Just for a moment." He places a soft kiss on my forehead and withdraws.

My pussy tightens around his cock as though desperate to keep him inside, but he pulls out, leaving me empty and quivering.

"I'll be right back," he says, the words sounding like a promise.

"I'll be waiting," I whisper, and melt into the furry coverlet.

My heart sinks a little as he retreats toward the exit, only to skip a beat when he pauses at the doorway and sighs.

"You're so beautiful, lying there all satisfied, exhausted, and full of my cum," he growls.

"Hurry back." I part my thighs.

He raises a hand. "Stay still. Don't spill a drop."

"Alright."

Another loud bang makes the lights flicker. Krampus growls and steps out into the hallway, letting the door swing shut.

As his hoofbeats retreat, I let my eyes flutter closed and smile. A warm breeze wafts in from the fireplace, making my skin tingle with anticipation.

I'm ready for whatever craziness comes next.

"Ho, ho, ho," says a deep voice.

My eyes snap open.

The most handsome man I've ever seen stands at the foot of the bed, and he's dressed like Father Christmas.

Chapter Fifteen

NATALIA

I scramble back toward the headboard, my feet digging into the mattress. The man standing at the foot of the bed is as tall as Krampus and maybe as broad, but he's completely human.

He can't be Father Christmas. Father Christmas is an old man with twinkling eyes, red cheeks, and a chubby dad body. The man standing over me is a silver fox with muscles.

"Who are you?" I whisper.

"Merry Christmas, Natalia." He walks around the bed and offers me a hand. "My name is Klaus."

I pull my knees toward my chest and wrap my arms around my shins. "Like Santa Claus?"

He grins. "I go by many names, but many call me Santa."

My gaze drops down to the proffered hand. Damn. "What's Father Christmas doing here?"

His grin widens, and he stretches his arms wide. "This is my home."

"Wait, are you the brother who imprisoned Krampus?"

"That's correct," he replies, his smile faltering. "My

brother and I have our differences, but I still love him dearly."

My jaw clenches. "How on earth can a man claim to love someone they kept in a dungeon for nearly a century?"

"It's complicated." Klaus sits on the edge of the mattress, making it dip.

I scoot further away, my heart pounding. Those blue eyes look kind, but I don't trust this guy—even if he claims to be Santa Claus. Most of the time, kindly exteriors are just a mask for an utter bastard.

"You were about to explain why you put your own brother in a dungeon," I say from between clenched teeth.

"His quarters beneath the house were comfortable," Klaus mutters. "The truth is, I had no choice. Krampus was too powerful, reckless, and destructive. He needed to be contained."

"So you could be the only Christmas deity?" I mutter back.

Klaus glances away, his lips thinning. "All children, no matter how wicked, deserve the opportunity to change their ways."

I glare at the side of his face. "How does leaving him in a dungeon help with that?"

"Krampus sees the evil in one's heart. He can tell if a child will become a mass murderer or the next evil dictator. If left unchecked Krampus will cleanse the world of all its wickedness."

"Wow, who would have thought Father Christmas would protect the evil?"

A muscle in his cheek flexes, and he flares his nostrils. My jaw tightens. Did Klaus think I would take his side because he's beautiful?

"My parents both died in Wizard War Four," I say.

He scratches his chin. "Pardon?"

"It was started by Doctor Ubel, a necromancer born in 1946, who killed thousands of innocent witches and wizards. A god like Krampus would have eliminated him at the first signs of showing evil."

Klaus sighs. "I am truly sorry for your loss, Natalia. I do understand your point. It's the reason I'm no longer standing in my brother's way."

This sounds like bullshit, considering Krampus had to escape. If Father Christmas was truly sorry he would have released his poor brother the moment he'd realized his mistake. Evil has been allowed to prosper, thanks to this arrogant bastard.

Angry words gather in the back of my throat. I want to spew them out at this creature in a tirade, but another warm breeze on my back reminds me that I'm completely naked.

Any false moves, and I'll be flashing Santa.

"Why are you here?"

Klaus takes a deep breath and scoots closer. "I came to see if you're enjoying your Christmas gift?"

"What do you mean—"

My jaw drops.

Every year, I send a message to Father Christmas, begging for a good man with a huge cock. Every year, he fails to deliver.

"Don't tell me it was you who sent Krampus to my apartment?" I ask.

"I tampered with the naughty list," he says with a deep chuckle. "Did my brother deliver your heart's desire?"

He looms so closely that I can smell his cologne—cinnamon, cloves, and pine. The heat radiating from his larger body makes my skin prickle. My cheeks burn, and I turn my head away. I'm not attracted to this guy. I'm happy with Krampus.

"You shouldn't be here," I mutter. "This is inappropriate."

"True," Klaus says, his voice soft. "But I must ask. Do you have any other wishes I can fulfill?"

"I—I can't think of anything. All I need is Krampus."

"I respect that." He places a large hand on my shoulder. "Let's get you dressed."

His touch is all happiness and warmth and Christmas cheer. Yesterday, I would have welcomed his advances. Today, I'm grinding my teeth. "Why would I allow another man to fetch me clothes when I'm perfectly happy with what I have?"

"Indeed?"

The teasing tone in his voice has me jerking away from his touch.

"You should leave," I say, my voice flat.

"I must say, your loyalty to my brother is admirable," he replies, the hand returning.

"It's not loyalty," I snap. "It's love."

Klaus grins, the corners of his eyes crinkling. "I believe you."

He looks so genuinely happy, it's hard to stay mad at him. And when even more warmth radiates through his palms and fills my heart, a smile tugs at the corners of my lips.

"Merry Christmas, Natalia."

The door slams open with a force that makes the room tremble. I turn toward the exit, expecting to see a disgruntled moose, but furry arms wrap around my waist and yank me off the bed.

"Krampus?" I squeak.

How on earth did he cross the room so quickly?

His deep growl reverberates against my back, making

every fine hair on my body stand on end. Oh shit. I hope the brothers aren't about to fight.

When Krampus places me in the corner and raises a magical barrier, my stomach drops.

Krampus charges across the room, leaving fiery hoof marks on the wooden floor, and slams into Klaus's chest with his horns. "Natalia belongs to me!"

A scream tears from my throat. At this rate, he'll kill his brother. I surge forward, but the barrier pushes me back. "Stop it!"

Klaus coughs out a mouthful of blood, staining his trim white beard. "It's not what it looks like, brother. I was simply—"

"No one looks at my Natalia."

He slashes his talons across Klaus's eyes, leaving behind deep gouges.

Krampus steps back, pulling his horns out of Klaus's chest. Klaus falls to his knees, clutching at his ravaged face.

I clap both hands over my mouth to suppress a scream.

"Oh, brother," Klaus says, his voice strained. "I didn't come here to start a fight."

Krampus grabs Klaus by the neck and slams him against the wall, causing an explosion of plaster. He closes a fist around his brother's hand and squeezes, filling the air with the sound of cracking bones.

My pussy throbs at the carnage, even though the extent of the violence makes me wince. No one has ever gotten jealous over me, let alone fought for my honor.

I want to tell Krampus that I'm his, that I could never find a man like Father Christmas attractive, but I'm too afraid to speak.

Klaus slumps against the wall, unconscious, and Krampus finally releases his grip. He turns to face me, and our eyes meet.

I'm expecting anger or rage, but instead, I'm met with a passionate, unbridled desire, as though he'd kill anyone who dared to touch me.

Klaus groans.

"Get out," Krampus snarls, his gaze possessive, fierce, and still fixed on mine.

Klaus mumbles and staggers to his feet and sighs. "I only came in to make sure that Natalia enjoyed her present."

Krampus drags his brother to the door. "You touched the woman I love."

My breath catches.

Love?

"Ho, ho, ho," says Klaus. "Perhaps my attempt at matchmaking compensates for locking you up. It was me who tampered with the naughty—"

"Out!" Krampus tosses his brother out into the hallway.

"I'll set a place for Natalia at Christmas lunch!" Klaus says.

Krampus slams the door shut, and the magical barrier dissipates. I walk to him on trembling legs, realizing that I'm wearing a white nightgown. At some point during our conversation, Klaus must have given me clothes.

"Did you mean it when you said you loved me?"

The words die in my throat when Krampus whirls around, his eyes blazing. "That was very naughty to allow my brother to touch what was mine," he says, his voice a low rumble. "Very naughty, indeed."

"What are you talking about?"

He stalks toward me, his hoofbeats striking the floor in counterpoint to my quickening pulse.

"Natalia, take off that nightgown. You're about to get your punishment."

Chapter Sixteen

KRAMPUS

One benefit of Klaus putting his filthy hand on my little witch is his ability to heal. My brother likes to mend broken things, and I'm sure he's already soothed Natalia's aching little pussy.

Cheeks reddening as I advance toward her, Natalia inches back toward the corner.

"Why should I be punished?" she asks, her eyes wide. "I didn't do anything wrong."

My cock stirs at her words, and I release a low chuckle. A little witch infused with Klaus's magic will make a very sturdy toy. One I can fuck without fear of killing.

"You allowed my brother to touch what's mine." I flash my teeth, enjoying how she squeezes her thighs together.

"What was I supposed to do? You left me defenseless and naked."

The sweet scent of her arousal fills my nostrils, making my cock push against its sheath. Natalia is my perfect submissive, both aroused and defiant at the prospect of being punished.

I cross the room in two hoofbeats and loom over her trembling frame. "Defiant as ever."

"K-Krampus..."

I reach out, tracing the outline of her lips with my finger. "Just because I'm punishing you doesn't mean I don't still love you."

"Oh fuck," Natalia whispers. "I love you, too."

Warmth fills my chest, making my heart swell to four times its usual size. For once in my entire existence, I'm hearing the words from someone other than that bastard, Klaus. I lean down, my tongue rolling out to meet her plump lips.

Natalia opens her mouth to accept me, and a moan escapes her as I plunder her mouth.

Mine.

She tastes of strawberries and wine, incense and spice, the promise of a love I never thought I'd find. Natalia is more than pleasure or pain or erotic delight—she fills the void—makes me complete.

"Undress," I command, my voice gruff.

She gazes up at me, her eyes heavy lidded, and pulls off the nightgown.

"Turn around."

She obeys and I gaze down at her perfect, round, unmarked ass. Any other time, I would throttle Klaus for removing the pretty patterns I made on her skin. Today, I'm just grateful for the chance to enjoy the woman I love.

As she turns back, my tongue slides down her hot cheek, over her neck, and toward the swell of her breast.

I flick her nipple with the tip of my tongue, making her whimper. She rocks forward, her body arching.

"So responsive," I murmur and lick a path to her other breast. As I circle the tight little bud, I notice two tiny holes.

"A piercing?" I ask.

She gives me an eager nod. "I have more."

"Show me."

Natalia leans against the wall and parts her thighs, revealing her wet pussy. I run the tips of my claws over her shoulder in a feather-light caress that makes her tremble.

"Are you dripping for me, Little Witch?"

"Yes, sir."

"Where are the piercings? I can't see them through all that delicious wetness."

Her cheeks darken. "One's on my clit." She taps the swollen little nub before sliding two fingers down her folds. "The other two are on my labia."

My cock jerks in response. I lean down and lock eyes with her, my tongue sliding between her swollen lips. She moans as I lap up her clit and savor her delicious taste.

"I'm going to hang something from them," I mumble around her folds.

Her lips twitch in a smile, and her eyes sparkle. Natalia obviously likes the idea.

"Do you want to cum?" I ask.

She squeezes her thighs, trapping the tip of my tongue. "More than anything."

"Then get on the table on your hands and knees, so I can decorate you for Christmas."

Natalia's mouth drops open, and her brows pull together as though confused. Before she can give me any sass, I growl, "Now."

She releases my tongue and scampers around the bed, to the round table on the other side of the room. After climbing up on its pinewood surface, she gets into position, displaying her curvaceous ass.

My poor cock pushes its way out from behind its sheath and drizzles precum. No amount of magic could force it back into its resting place at the prospect of fucking Natalia from behind.

"Beautiful," I say, my hand cupping one rounded ass cheek. "Will you stay still and let me dress you as my Christmas tree?"

"How?" she asks.

I reach down, tweak her nipple between my thumb and forefinger, and grin at the way she shivers. "First, I'll hang baubles from your nipples and clit. Then I'll lace up the piercings in your labia with jingle bells attached to shiny threads."

"And then?" she asks, her voice trembling with anticipation.

"When I've teased your clit until you can no longer cum, I'll roll you onto your back, wrap those pretty legs with Christmas lights and tinsel, and point your ankles to the ceiling. I'll tie a golden star to your feet, surround you with presents, and fill your pussy with my huge cock."

Natalia moans louder, her hips bucking. Arousal trickles down her inner thighs, making my mouth water.

The erotic image of her trussed up like a Christmas tree makes me lightheaded. My balls draw up as though readying themselves to cum. I grind my teeth and force back the surge of lust. Natalia deserves a Christmas fucking she'll never forget.

"You mentioned safe words, earlier," I say. "If anything I do tonight is too much, or too painful, simply say 'red' and I will cease."

"But I want it all," Natalia moans.

"And you'll get it," I reply. "But we need safe words in case you change your mind or become overwhelmed."

"No chance of that happening." She turns around, fixing me with bright eyes. "I want you to wrap me up like a Christmas present and fuck me until I see stars."

My cock throbs in response, and I take a deep breath. Time to turn my naughty little sub into a sexy Christmas tree.

"Open your legs," I rasp.

She parts her knees.

"Wider."

My tongue drags up her slit, making her legs tremble. I raise a hand to summon Christmas decorations from all corners of the house.

This will probably mess up Klaus's Christmas display, but he has an entire army of elves ready to clean up any mess.

After giving Natalia a spank that makes her ass cheek jiggle, I move around to her side and pull at her nipple. She hisses through her teeth.

I thread a thin silk ribbon through her nipple piercing and attach it to a red bauble. Natalia groans as it weighs down her breast.

"How does that feel?" I pull on the sphere, giving her nipple a gentle stretch.

"It feels amazing," she replies, her voice thick. "Please do the other one, Sir."

I attach a green bauble to the right breast and feel around her belly button for another hole. The tip of my claw catches on a piercing, and I thread a golden ribbon through it before suspending a silver snowflake.

"There." I tie a string of tinsel around her waist, conjure it into a bow, and step back to admire my handiwork. "Now you're halfway to becoming a Christmas fuck tree."

Natalia pants. "When do I get your cock?"

"Any more from you, and you'll get my tongue up your ass," I growl.

"P-please."

I walk around to her spread legs, only to find her pussy

wetter than before. It takes every effort not to start feasting on her juices. Instead, I lick a stripe down her lower back, past her pucker, and stop at her taint.

Natalia's breath quickens as I circle her asshole with my tongue. I part her round cheeks and slather her with enough saliva to lubricate what I'm about to do next.

"Remember how I fucked your tight little pussy with my tongue?" I ask.

"Yes," she whispers.

"I'm going to stretch out your ass a little bit before slipping in a plug."

Her asshole tightens beneath my tongue. "Please."

I lick a slow circle around her hole, making her moan for more. A deep chuckle resounds in my chest, making my cock throb. Who would have thought Natalia would have such a sensitive little opening?

Her asshole loosens a little, enough for me to fill her with my tongue. Her anal passage tightens around me, making my cock jealous. Natalia gasps and trembles as I slide further into her back passage, active every inch the perfect submissive.

"Good girl," I say, my words garbled. "You look so beautiful with my tongue halfway up your ass."

Natalia whines and whimpers, seeming too lost in pleasure to speak. I pull out a little, enjoying how her anus tightens.

"What do you want?" I ask. "Use your words."

"P-please bugger me with your thick tongue," she mumbles.

"Louder."

She repeats herself, making me moan and thrust my tongue further into her asshole. Natalia comes undone, crying out and bucking against me as I stretch her tight opening. I torment her more, licking and thrusting in time with her moans. Just when I think she can't take anymore, Natalia pushes back against my tongue and cums hard.

I pull out of her ass, lap up her fluids, and sigh.

"What a good little witch. Now you're loose enough for the Christmas toy."

I conjure a rubber butt plug shaped like a Christmas tree and slip it into Natalia's tight little asshole. She bucks and groans as it slides in, but her greedy little ass gobbles it up. The bauble at the end lights up like Rudolph's red nose.

"Turn around and lie on your back," I growl.

She flips around on the table and gets into position with her legs spread, looking like a Christmas banquet.

"Spread those legs further," I say, lowering my voice into a deep command. "Once I've decorated that pretty little pussy of yours, I'm going to stuff it full of my cock."

Chapter Seventeen

NATALIA

I lie on my back, still dazed from an earth-shattering climax. Krampus stares down at me, his eyes ablaze. The long tongue that reamed my asshole lolls halfway down his chest, making me groan.

Fucking hell. Who would have thought I could orgasm from anal? Even though my asshole is stuffed full of rubber, my pussy clamps and spasms, desperate to be filled.

I part my thighs, still shuddering from that orgasm. Krampus's rumbling growl reminds me to open my legs.

"Dirty girl," he rumbles. "Look at the mess you've made of your pussy. Someone's going to have to clean it up."

"Clean me, sir, please," I whisper.

That long, thick tongue swipes down my slit, causing my entire body to shiver. I'm not sure how much of this teasing I can take when I'm so desperate for his cock.

Bells jingle from all sides of the room. I raise my head to find tiny silver objects flying into his large hands.

"What are you doing, sir?" I ask.

"Decorating my Christmas cunt. Now, hold onto your knees and bring them to your chest."

I bite down on my bottom lip, doing exactly as he says, and exposing myself fully to his regard. Krampus crouches between my spread legs and holds my labia between his claws.

"Look at how beautiful you are," he says, his voice breathy with wonder.

He threads something slippery and soft into my clit piercing, and I glance down to find it's a thin, red ribbon. The fabric slides down, weaving itself into my labia piercings before he attaches the bells.

My entire pussy feels so alive. I'm so desperate and aroused that each of his touches makes me cry out for more.

"Please," I whisper. "I need you right now."

"Patient little witches get Krampus's cock. Impatient ones get spankings."

His words send a thrill down my spine, and I moan, "Can't I have both?"

After giving my ass a swat that sends vibrations to my clit, he steps back, seeming to admire his work.

"How is it?" I ask.

He summons a mirror and hovers it between my legs.

Two sets of red ribbons weave between the labia piercings, attached to stars and silver bells. At the top is a sprig of mistletoe.

"Nobody has ever decorated my pussy."

"Nobody ever will get to adorn what's mine," he snarls.

Warmth fills my chest as I bask in his fiery gaze. I love that he's so possessive.

"Yours," I murmur. "And thank you for this. It's beautiful."

"It's nothing compared to the beauty of your soul."

Krampus steps forward, his eyes burning with desire. "Nothing compared to the beauty of your submission."

My breath catches. He's so intense, so powerful, so passionate. I'm trembling so hard that I can barely keep my legs open.

With a flick of his fingers, he conjures the ribbons to part my labia even further, eliciting the most exquisite stretch.

"I planned on fucking you with your legs trussed like a Christmas tree, but now I need to see into your soul."

"How?" I whisper.

He points a claw at the corner of his eye and gestures down at mine. "Eye contact. Will you allow me to connect our souls while we fuck?"

Earlier, when I rode his cock, I thought I glimpsed the loneliness of his past. It stretched out for eons, making my own isolation feel like a momentary blip. Now I'm ready to look again, to let him see the depth of my soul, and the depth of my submission.

"Yes," I say, my voice firming. "I want to feel your soul."

"Scoot to the edge of the table and keep your legs spread."

I shuffle toward him, my gaze raking down his muscular form to his outrageously huge erection. Dread coils in my gut as I contemplate its length and the fact that it's shaped like an L.

The last time we had sex, I had been on top. I had controlled the rhythm, the pace, and the amount of cock my pussy could sheathe. I only took in the smaller part of the L.

"W-wait a minute." I release my knees and hold out both palms. "Your cock is too big. It would tear me apart."

His eyes blaze, and I hold my breath, waiting for him to bellow something like, 'You asked for my cock and now you're going to enjoy it!'

Instead, he places both hands on my knees and leans down, so our gazes connect. "Natalia," he rumbles. "When my brother was in this room, did he touch you?"

Guilt squeezes my heart, and I jerk my head to the side. "He did, but it was only the shoulder. Krampus, you've got to believe me, I would never—"

"Hush, Little Witch. I am not accusing you of being untrue."

I turn my head to find his eyes shining with love.

"Klaus is an asshole, but he's also a very powerful healer. He knows that sex with me can be deadly, and his touch would prepare you for my crooked cock."

"You think I can take it all?"

"I know you can."

My teeth worry at my bottom lip, making him frown.

"We'll go slow, and I'll make sure you're comfortable, but at the first sign of pain, use your safe word."

"Yes, sir," I say, my heart fluttering at his tenderness. "I trust you."

His long tongue swipes at my lips, and I open my mouth to deepen the kiss. The fire in his eyes screams that he wants this connection perhaps even more than I do. He wants me to survive this fuck.

Krampus tightens his grip on my knees and shoves them further apart. The blunt tip of his cock pushes at my entrance, and I whimper.

"Here it comes," he says, his voice a low growl. "Are you ready to take my huge cock?"

My breath hitches, but I manage to nod and add, "Please."

I'm so slippery and wet and needy that he slides in, inch by exquisite inch, until I'm stretched to my limit. He pauses for a moment, giving me a chance to adjust. My muscles flutter around his thick cockhead, and the shorter part of his erection, but we both know there's plenty more.

"Natalia, you're doing so well," he says.

I reach up to grip his furry hands as he pushes into me, stretching my entrance even further. The sensation is so intense that I cry out, and Krampus stops moving until I'm able to relax again.

Bloody hell.

I'm taking in the other side of his cock.

"Good girl," he murmurs and pushes inside me a few more inches.

Pleasure and pain mingle in my core, making me bite down on my lip. My clit swells, feeling like it's doubled in size, and my pussy won't stop clamping around his girth.

"How does it feel, pet?" Krampus asks, his voice heavy with arousal.

"Blissful," I moan, my eyes sliding shut.

"Eyes on me," he says. "I want to see you come apart around my cock."

Tears prickle my eyes at the intensity of the sensation, but each slide takes me to higher levels of ecstasy. Whatever Klaus did to me earlier is allowing me to take the huge cock that's claiming me as its own.

Over the next several minutes, he slides into me, each gentle thrust making the bells attached to my labia tinkle. My breath turns shallow as I take in more and more of Krampus as though my organs have shrunk to accommodate his monster dick.

"You're mine, Natalia," he rasps.

"Yours," I repeat. "But why have we stopped?"

"Look down."

I rise to my elbows and glance between my legs to find him sheathed to the hilt. "What?"

"You see that?" He grins. "Your greedy little pussy has swallowed me up."

"Wow," I moan.

"Now, I'm going to fill you with my cum."

Krampus pulls out, but his cock is so big and bendy that the process takes longer than usual. My walls flutter around his girth, feeling every vein, every contour, every ridge. Sparks of pleasure skitter up and down my spine, making my toes curl.

He holds my chin between his claws with a movement so tender that it makes my heart flip. "I'm going to take you nice and easy until you loosen around my girth."

"Yes," I whisper.

"After that, I'll ride you nice and hard."

Krampus thrusts. As promised, the movements are slow and exquisite. Sweat beads on my brow and across my skin, but he dries it off with his long, thick tongue.

Each gentle snap of his hips makes the bells attached to my labia ring, and the mistletoe tethered to my clit bounces back and forth. The soft berries and leaves brush against my sensitive nub, pushing me closer to the edge.

Krampus takes his time, easing me with the pleasure that comes with each stroke. His hips roll, and my nerve endings flare like Christmas lights.

Pressure gathers behind my clit before I know it, and my entire lower half quivers. I release a hoarse moan. This is more pleasure than I can handle.

"I love the way you squeeze my shaft," he says. "I love the way you take all of me and mewl for more."

"Yes, more," I groan.

"I love the way you flutter every time I go balls deep," he growls.

"Krampus, I'm so close. Please, don't stop."

He continues to thrust until I'm screaming his name,

and my climax shatters around him like Christmas fireworks. Sparks dance across my vision in an array of red and green and gold.

Molten pleasure explodes in my belly and stretches out across my limbs. I've never had a full-body orgasm, but then I've never taken the full might of a god.

Krampus speeds up, pushing into me with a strength that nearly breaks me apart. I buck against his thrusts, squeezing down that juicy cock as the orgasm propels me higher and higher. His name is the only thing I can utter as my eyes roll to the back of my head.

"Fuck, Natalia," he growls. "At this rate, I'll drown you in cum."

"Please," I say between ragged breaths. "Fill me up."

His cock pulses once, twice, three times, before he throws his head back, roars, and floods my pussy with ropes of hot fluid. My muscles latch onto his thick shaft twitching and milking him for every drop.

When I come down from my high, Krampus lifts me off the table and carries me across the room. My eyelids become heavy as he lays me down on the fur coverlet, and I drift into a deep sense of contentment, secure in the knowledge that I'm loved.

Krampus gets on the bed beside me and pulls me into his chest, his larger body forming a cocoon of safety.

"Will you take my mark?" he asks.

"What does that mean?" I murmur.

"It's a sigil a god can place on his devotee that extends their life. You'll be able to summon me from the human world or transport yourself to my side. With my marking, you will never grow old or weak."

"You'd do that for me?"

"I would keep you here forever, where you would never age or die, but you want to explore your mortal life."

"For now," I murmur. "But I'll still take your mark."

His satisfied rumble makes my heart soar.

"You belong to me, Natalia," he says, making gentle scratches on my arm with the tip of his claw. "My lover, my submissive, my little witch. Mine forever."

"Forever."

I relax into his embrace and sigh, feeling like I'm the heroine of a fairytale. Every year, I begged Santa for a man with a huge cock, when what I really wanted was a monster who could love me until the end of time.

Who knew Christmas wishes could come true?

Epilogue

CHRISTMAS EVE
   FIVE YEARS LATER

I walk around the attic apartment that's been my home since I turned eighteen and say goodbye to every corner. My clothes and books and trinkets are all packed up and transported to the North Pole.

The baby kicks, reminding me of the biggest change in my life. I rub my belly, marveling at the miracle growing inside me.

Krampus's mark gave me more than the ability to summon him—I'm more powerful than the average witch and have enough magic to carry his child.

According to the magical ultrasound, our son looks like a regular infant, but Klaus assures us he will be born with the abilities of a demigod.

It feels natural to move in with Krampus and start a new life at the North Pole with him and our son.

My phone rings. I glance at the screen to find that it's Krampus.

"Where are you?" he asks.

"Just finishing." My gaze flicks to the clock. 11:51. "Don't tell me you've completed your duties already?"

"I have one more name on the naughty list, then I'm free to join you."

Laughing, I shake my head. "Hurry up because I'm aching for my Christmas fuck."

Krampus hangs up, leaving me staring at the blank screen. I slip my phone into the pocket of my cloak and walk to the final corner.

Flames burst from the fireplace, making me stagger back. Krampus steps out in a shower of sparks, grinning like a lunatic.

He's as imposing as ever, standing over seven feet tall excluding his horns. Despite the flashing of fangs and the wicked glint in his eye, he's still the same man I fell in love with at Christmas five years ago.

Krampus's heavy hoofbeats echo across the empty room, making my skin tingle.

"What happened to the last name on the naughty list?" I place my hands on my hips.

He waves a dismissive claw. "I dispatched him to hell"

"Krampus!"

He pulls me into his arms and sweeps me off my feet. "The young man had a corrupt soul. No amount of birching could have stopped him from becoming a mass murderer."

"Really?" I narrow my eyes.

"On a god's honor," he growls.

"Who am I to question the great Krampus?" I throw my arms around his neck. "Must be exhausting, being so powerful and all-knowing."

"My reward is you." Krampus grins, his fangs glinting in the firelight.

We stand there in the flickering warmth, Krampus holding me close while I cling to him like a lifeline.

"Merry Christmas, my love." He brings his mouth to mine for a lingering kiss. "Thank you for the best ever gift."

"Thank you for being such a great Dom and giving me a family," I murmur against his lips.

Krampus pulls back to look into my eyes. "I love you, now and forever."

"I love you too."

"Come on." Krampus waves a hand and opens a portal into our North Pole bedroom, where a crackling fire awaits. "Let's go home."

About the Author

I write dark contemporary and paranormal romance featuring villains, monsters, morally gray heroes, and the women who make them feral.

When I'm not writing steamy scenes, you'll probably find me at my TikTok, @SiggyShade

Join my newsletter for exclusive short stories and updates on upcoming books: www.siggyshade.com/newsletter

Also by Siggy Shade

Paranormal Romance:

Tentacle Entanglement

Jack's Head

Stalked by the Boogie Man

Swallowing Water

Contemporary Romance

Wicked Lessons

Printed in Great Britain
by Amazon

34550655R00081